Asunder

Asunder

Eric Lee Bowers

THIRD WORLD PRESS
Chicago

Third World Press
Publishers since 1967

First Third World Press Edition published 2004
Originally published by New Millennium Books 1999
Printed in the United States of America

This novel is a work of fiction. Names, characters, places and incidents either are the product of the author's imagination or are used fictitiously. Any resemblance to actual persons, living or dead, events or locales is entirely coincidental.

Library of Congress Cataloging-in-Publication Data
Asunder by Eric Lee Bowers.
 p. cm.
 ISBN 0-88378-254-5 (alk. paper)
l. African American families—Fiction 2. Loss(Psychology—fiction
I.Title.
PS3602.0896A88 2004
813' .6-dc22

            2002073285
         08 07 06 05 04 12345

For All my Family and Friends
And Friends who have become Family

...And they twain shall be one flesh: so then they are no more twain, but one flesh. What therefore God hath joined together, let no man put asunder.

Matthew 19:6

One

He had once heard someone ask, "What color is the pain?" as if pain could be surmised in hues of red and amber. At the time he thought the concept was ridiculous, something conceived by some desperate artist staring blankly onto a canvas and hoping desperately to pull the colors of anguish from a palette filled with bright pastels and thick gooey oils. *What color is the pain?* he thought as he bit down hard on his lower lip and closed his eyes tight. That's when it came to him in a wash of bright orange with streaks of red and tips of sharp yellow. Yes, he thought, pain definitely does have a color, and the colors were now consuming him.

The throbbing sensation had reached a place beyond pain. It felt as if something had ruptured somewhere behind his right kneecap and was now hemorrhaging its way into his upper thigh. He felt his leg swelling, like a balloon being filled with water, and soon, he didn't know how much longer it would take, but soon, it would invariably explode, covering him and everything and everyone around him in bright red. Red...the color of pain. Blood red, true pain. He could see the silhouette of the desperate artist in his head dipping his hands into pools of rich dark blood and smearing them along the blank white pristine canvas. His mind was rambling now. He had to focus. Somehow, he had to fight his way back from the pain. He had a sudden primal urge to scream, but he managed to hold it back. He didn't want to bring any attention to himself. He didn't want either of the paramedics working in the back of the speeding ambulance to turn their attention away from the woman lying on the gurney. Chance bit down a little harder on his lower lip and pushed back against the inner wall of the ambulance as he tried to shift his weight and ease some of the pressure building within his leg. *It's gonna blow!* he thought, a ruptured shank spewing out crimson like a fire hose. Even as this thought crossed his mind, his eyes never shifted from the woman lying on the gurney across from him.

Hang on sweetheart, he thought silently, trying to send her whatever strength he had left. The screaming siren had become a low drone. The world outside seemed to pass by in a slow motion blur. Who ever would have thought an ambulance had to abide by the posted speed limit. How could one have ever known that those annoying blaring sirens that interrupt your day to day travels and force you to pull to the side or miss a light at an intersection could one day be your ride against time? Everything was just taking too long, and time was running out. It's amazing how your concept of time will change depending upon your situation, Chance thought to himself. He thought they had all the time in the world. An entire lifetime together. There would be plenty of time to say the forgotten "I love you" or a regretful "I'm sorry." There would be plenty of time to make up for that time not spent together because of a hectic schedule and busy lifestyle. They were young and there was so much time ahead of them. The future was all theirs, or so they thought.

But as Chance sat in the back of the speeding ambulance, the realization that nothing in life is guaranteed rushed around him like a cold bitter wind in a harsh winter storm. The woman he loved was dying, and there was nothing in the world anyone could do to change that. *Please, just hold on,* he thought once more as he stared at her.

Her eyes were closed slightly, but not in a peaceful sort of way. It was that half-mast, empty stare that he had seen once before. That look people get as the soul within them searches for a way out. "I love you," he wanted to tell her. *Things are going to get better, I promise,* his mind continued. *Just please don't leave me.*

She seemed to hear his thoughts as her eyes shifted towards him. There was a slight twitch tugging at the side of her mouth, as if she were trying to smile and say, "Don't worry, everything is going to be okay." Then, suddenly, she coughed and a flood of red sprang from her rich full lips. Some of the blood filled spittle landed on the face of the paramedic leaning over her.

"Goddamn it, she's hemorrhaging!" the paramedic barked as he craned his neck to wipe the blood from his cheek onto his crisp white shirt. His partner, a young blonde woman with a face that looked more like a cover girl's than a paramedic, glanced back at Chance, perhaps realizing that there may have been a bit too much distress in her partner's voice.

"How's the leg, Mr. Williams?" she asked, trying to shift the attention away from the scene.

"I'm fine," Chance managed, still trying to repress the scream of anguish scratching at the back of his throat. "Just take care of her."

"Doing all we can," the other paramedic finished without glancing in Chance's direction. "We'll be there shortly."

It was at that moment that Chance realized he was about to loose the only thing he had ever loved.

Two

D r. Marsha Wysse sat in the Emergency Room doctor's lounge staring at the stark white wall in front of her and going over the events of the evening. There were still six hours left on her night shift, and right now, it seemed as if time stood still. She glanced up at the oversized clock on the wall and watched the pencil-thin line of a second hand glide smoothly past the bold black numbers. It did appear to be working, although she could swear that it had been 10:59 fifteen minutes ago the last time she had glanced at that very same clock.

All and all, it had been a pretty uneventful night, considering that Sunday nights were usually the time weekend warriors came pouring in, touting aches, cuts, bruises and broken bones. A time when all the hypochondriacs in town crawled out of the woodwork and claimed every illness known to man, hoping they wouldn't have to report to work Monday morning. A night when the aged seemed to trade their Sunday meals at retirement homes for holding up in the ER waiting room, complaining of chest pains and labored breathing. Dr. Wysse wondered if this had anything to do with the fact that families usually visited their old on Sundays, and when that visit was over, the pain those old hearts felt was actually the pain of loneliness and rejection. The thought was fleeting and could not replace her sense of how quiet this evening was. Almost too quiet.

She remembered tending to the woman who had decided to add the tip of her index finger to the salad she had been chopping for her family. And the little boy who had fallen from the park's towering monkey bars while sticking out his tongue and playing "You can't catch me..." The poor tyke had fractured his arm in two places and nearly bitten his "Now-or-Later" coated tongue in half. But, other than that, there hadn't been much to speak of. She pondered calling her husband again to see if he had tucked their two-year-old son in for the night, but realized that it was much too late and that, of course, he had. All considered, it had been a very quiet evening. And then all hell broke loose.

The gurney hit the ER double doors with such force it sounded as though someone had just fired a cannon. The thunderous sound sent a chill up the young doctor's spine that lingered somewhere at the base of her skull. She started running even before her feet hit the ground. Every ER emergency drill came flooding back into her mind. She noted on her way out of the lounge that the clock on the wall was indeed running. The race against time had started and she was already a few steps behind.

"One one thousand, two one thousand, three one thousand...Come on, Roberta, breathe!" yelled the female paramedic straddling the woman on the gurney. "Stay with us, girl. Don't give up." She continued to administer the sharp and sudden blows, one hand over the other, to the woman's chest while her partners in paramedic blue pushed the gurney down the hallway as quickly as they could. The squeaky wheels of the gurney scraped against the hospital's brightly polished floor, creating a sound that was reminiscent of fingernails on a chalkboard.

"Whadda we got?" Dr. Wysse asked, joining the quick moving entourage.

"Multiple contusions, fractures, concussion and severe internal hemorrhaging," one of the medics responded. "You name it, it's either broken or bleeding." Dr. Wysse quickly switched places with the young paramedic straddling the woman and continued the CPR.

"I need some vitals here!" Dr. Wysse shrieked. "And get me a team in Trauma 7 STAT!" The walls and floor flew by in an off-white blur. She couldn't help noticing the soft and gentle face of the young woman underneath her on the gurney, an unconscious black woman with short, jet-black hair that framed her face perfectly. Her skin was the color of rich mahogany, and her cheek-bones rode high and proud. Many African Americans make claims about having "Indian in their blood," but this woman definitely had her share. It was hard to tell now, but underneath the swollen bruises and caked blood, Roberta Williams was quite beautiful.

The doctor stared down at the young woman's face. She wondered what it would be like to see this lovely human being smile again. She imagined the warm satisfaction she would have if she could just patch this woman back together, take away the pain and send her home with the promise that everything was going to be all right. But the cold, dead stare in Roberta's light brown eyes said something else. It was a stare of good-bye, the peaceful, empty stare people get when they drop all their worldly burdens and start to walk down that long corridor into the realm of bright white light.

"Don't you give up on me!" Dr. Wysse yelled. "What's her name? Did anybody get her name?"

"Roberta..." Chance called out from the foot of the gurney. "Her name is Roberta."

Dr. Wysse turned to Chance and came face to face with a pair of the saddest eyes she had ever seen. They held adoration and pain, love and anguish. For some reason she stopped and stared momentarily at him. Somehow she knew, just in that brief instant as she looked into those desperate eyes, the man before her would never be the same.

Chance Williams, who had disowned his birth name of Eugene Brice years ago, was hobbling alongside the growing crowd. He was a tall, thin man, with muscles that flexed as he moved. His dark skin was the color of glistening sweet syrup. Not the maple-flavored crap, but the rich dark color of molasses. His eyes were a deep dark brown floating in sorrowful pools of red. Those eyes, seen on better days, could be enchantingly hypnotic. But right now, they were just very sad and desperate.

The sad eyes stared at Dr. Wysse, pleading with her to save the young life on the gurney. The doctor skipped a beat of her pounding on Roberta's chest and lost herself in Chance's eyes. The entourage quickly began to fall into place as they moved past the doors of Trauma Room Number Seven.

"I'm sorry sir," Chance heard a droning voice say in the background. "You can't be in here."

Groping hands touched and pushed him. Cold and unfeeling hands that tried to show him the way out. "I'm not leaving!" Chance argued, his outstretched fingers straining to take hold of Roberta's limp hand. "That's my wife, and I'm not leaving her side!"

Dr. Wysse saw the look in Chance's eyes. It was a look that said, "I ain't letting go no matter what you say." She had seen that look before and knew there was no time to argue with it right now. It was the same look those big ol' fat women at sad funerals get when they throw themselves on top of the casket and scream, "That's my baby!" There's no use fighting with that kind of outpour. Besides, someone might get hurt in the process. The only thing to do is stand back and watch it flow.

"Stand back, sir," a nurse said, pushing a device that looked like a space-age, super-charged portable TV set on wheels.

"I'm getting two heartbeats," Dr. Wysse announced with a warning tone. "We've got an expectant mother here, people, let's step it up. Get me a fetal monitor and a preemie ICU down here fast! And find out who's on Pediatrics Emergency, I want them here now!"

She glanced back at Chance, who had now been pushed into the background. He wanted, no *needed*, to be in there, but his presence was only making her more uncomfortable. She noticed his eyes following hers as she looked up at the monitor in front of her. The screen was blank. "Why the hell don't I have anything on this monitor yet?"

Chance watched every move intensely. His eyes refused to blink or turn away. The sounds inside the trauma room became muffled, as if he were sinking under deep and murky waters. His eyes stung to a point beyond pain. He thought if he could just blink it would all be over. Maybe if he could just close his eyes he could wake up back at home in his bed, lying next to Roberta. He would hold her close and kiss her ear, gently guiding his tongue in and around the crevasses. She'd shutter, giggle and tell him to stop, but she wouldn't pull away and he wouldn't stop. Then she would turn to him and their lips would meet tenderly. If he could just close his eyes now...but he couldn't. He had apparently forgotten how to blink, and he couldn't take his eyes off the woman he loved. The mother of his unborn child. The woman who lay on the blood-soaked bed and fought for her life.

Goddammit, he thought. *If only we had left when we wanted to. If we just had not listened to Michael.*

Three

The blaring pipe organ from the amusement park's Ferris wheel drowned out all other sounds in the park. The overbearing "umm paa paa" and disconnected melodies sounded like air escaping out of a ragged set of bagpipes while mariachis played "La Cucaracha" on loud, tinny horns. It was a hot and sticky afternoon, one of those days when the sun seemed to follow you no matter where you were, to beat down on you relentlessly until you were a mass of sweaty, sticky flesh. One of those days that makes you rank ice cream right up there with orgasms. "That's what I want," Roberta thought out loud as she left the park's port-a-potty. "A nice big triple scoop ice cream cone."

"Ya gotta be kidding me," Michael responded. His face was lost somewhere between outrageous laughter and a confused grimace. "You've either been eating or peeing ever since we got here. I thought we were gonna ride something." Chance and Roberta's friend Michael was a muscular, stocky, handsome man with a squared chin and a boyish face. He had eyes like a fawn's and lashes every woman yearned for. His smile was radiant. He had learned at a young age how to capture the sunlight in that bright smile and charm his way through anything. Right now, that smile was working its magic on Roberta.

"You try having something growing inside of you for seven months and see how you handle it," Roberta snapped back. She had a "get the hell outta my way" look on her face as she pushed past him and continued to waddle toward the concession stands. Roberta had just entered her third trimester of pregnancy, and, already, she could feel the additional weight starting to pull on her like loads of wet sand. She was always hungry and always thinking of what she would eat next, even while she was chowing down on the meal in front of her. And, incredibly, her biggest fear was getting fat. This pregnancy thing had her jumping through emotional hoops. But it was a feeling she wouldn't trade for the world.

Roberta and Chance had all but given up on having a child. They had tried for three years straight and except for a brief glimmer of hope that ended in an early miscarriage, thought they were destined to live out the rest of their lives as the childless couple people would point to at parties with a barely audible whisper, "There they go. Ain't it a shame...and they would've made such good parents too."

Their sex life had become more of a chore than anything else, with all the painful procedures, ovulation tests, basal charts and the ever-present thermometer next to the bed to measure any hint of ovulation before every attempt at intercourse. They had even been instructed to limit their sexual activity to one position—the missionary position that allowed for optimum penetration of spermatic deposits. Roberta had a difficult time getting worked up for sex when it was dissected in such technical terms. Many times they just ended the act with an exchange of empty glances that resembled a handshake. It was like saying, "Good job, nice effort, hope it works." Then they'd just roll over, back to back, and fall asleep. The whole ordeal had made their lives cold and barren, perhaps even more than having no child at all.

The rigors of conception had started to take their toll on Chance as well. That was all he could think about while he sat in the cold and empty, over-sanitized examination room where he and his wife had gone for fertility tests. The room was dimly lit with pale sand colored walls adorned with lifeless paintings of flowers and landscapes. There was not much furniture to speak of, a couple of thick cushioned wing back chairs and a matching sofa each had an end table placed next to them holding a stack of men's magazines and boxes of tissue. A twenty-seven inch television set and a VCR sat in the center of the room, with a rack of porno videotapes placed neatly nearby. Chance sat alone in the room in one of the wing back chairs, closing his eyes tying to mentally remove himself from the surroundings. The sweet, stinging smell of disinfectant irritated his nose and tickled the back of his throat, sending him into a sneezing fit.

"Are you all right in there, sweetheart?" Roberta asked beyond the closed door.

"I'm fine," he responded. "I'll be out in a minute." But he wasn't fine at all. In fact, he was damn near hyperventilating. It was the first time, to his knowledge, that he had sat alone in a room and beat his meat while his wife, several nurses and a doctor waited anxiously outside for the results. He tried to concentrate, tried to find something that could help him along. The magazines on the table did absolutely no good, and he was too embarrassed to turn on the video. The image of the cute little nurse with the large breasts who greeted them when they arrived floated into his mind. But that image was quickly replaced by one of Roberta waiting in the hallway, tapping her foot impatiently and nervously checking her watch. Chance closed his eyes tight and thought of something else—a dark, secret image with wild and ravenous passion. The thought did the trick.

Chance was relieved when the test results came back saying that his sperm count was more than adequate. There was nothing wrong with him, nor was there any problem with Roberta. They were told to just keep trying.

One morning a few months later, Chance was sleeping soundly when Roberta burst into the room. She had climbed on top of him like a rider mounting a stallion.

"Okay, okay," Chance had muttered through a cloudy, sleepy haze, and without thinking, started to remove his boxers.

"No need for that Papa," Roberta had chimed. "We did it!" They had embraced as a wave of excitement washed over the two of them. "But since you have it out anyway," Roberta had added. "Care to celebrate?" And then, for the first time in three years, without necessity, without a deliberate purpose, they had made love.

"Okay, check it out, people," Michael announced, unfolding a map of the carnival. "Here's a ride directly across from a restroom. It's like nirvana! Now we can ride something, and Ms. Peebody here can go check out another port-a-potty. What more could we want outta life, huh?"

"You could shut up once in a while," Roberta said. "That would be an improvement."

Michael wrapped his muscular arm around Roberta's shoulders and led her off across the park.

"But what about my ice cream?" Roberta whined.

"What's the point?" answered Michael. "You're just gonna pee it out five minutes from now."

Chance looked through the lens of his brand new Nikon S-35 camera. He snapped a few shots of Michael and Roberta walking in the distance. The camera's auto-winder whirled with a *click-pssst, click-pssst.* Chance loved the sound and the creative rush he got whenever he lifted the instrument to his eye. He turned to Michael's wife, Lauren, and framed her face to fill the lens. His artistic eye couldn't resist the vision. She looked at him with round eyes that seemed almost too large for her soft and delicate face. Her eyes could melt the coldest heart, and her smile could set it ablaze once more. Only five feet and two inches tall and with a frame that could define petite, she looked like a child. But no child could ever be this radiant. *Click-psst-click-psst,* the camera hummed, capturing her radiant beauty and transferring it to 35mm frames.

Chance lowered his camera and followed Lauren's eyes to Roberta and Michael. "Why is it that whenever those two get together, I feel like I need a striped shirt and a whistle?" Chance asked, watching them bantering. "Shall we join them?" he said, offering Lauren his arm in a gallant sort of way. Lauren simply looked at him with those big, deep, penetrating eyes.

"Offsides," she responded. Her voice had a warning tone. It was the tone of your mother's voice when she says your name softly for the last time just before she picks up that thin, razor sharp, red extension cord and starts whipping your ass. *"Eugene... didn't I warn you?"* Chance could hear a stern voice echo in the back of his head. He quickly shook off the memory and followed Lauren's lead.

The sun had started to abandon them, leaving to heat some other part of the world and giving way to the cold chill of the night air. The nights in the small, lazy town of Petersburg had a way of suddenly turning cold, and the breeze off the water made people want to cuddle closer to those they held near to their hearts. Chance moved behind Roberta and wrapped his long, strong arms around her. He kissed her gently on the cheek. The cold air gave her a sudden chill. She shuddered. "You okay?" he asked. She nodded and smiled.

Lauren stood nearby, also shuddering from the cold. An angry scowl had now taken the place of her bright smile and deep dimples. Michael could be so insensitive at times she thought. It angered her to discover that tonight would be one of those nights. Michael was mentally gone, totally engrossed by one of the park's carnival game booths. The game was one of those where the players must toss a Cheerio-like disk over and around the neck of one of the soda pop bottles that sat on the floor. It didn't matter to Michael that the hole in the disk was barely large enough to fit around the bottle, or that the bottles were placed so close together that each one protected the others from any chance of a ringer. It didn't even matter that he was now down thirty bucks and had run out of cash. He had worked himself up to a fevered pitch and was going to beat this game or go broke trying.

"Somebody give me two more dollars," Michael demanded, pulling his hand out of his pocket flecked with the small tufts of lint. "I almost had it!"

"Yeah, but that was two hours and thirty dollars ago," Roberta reminded him.

"Hey, I'm trying to win your kid his first stuffed animal," Michael claimed. "Work with me."

"You know what, Michael?" Lauren started in. "You're becoming a real pain in the ass!"

"Oh, I'm a pain in the ass?" Michael snapped back. "I thought we were supposed to be having a good time. You're the one with the stick shoved up your ass. But oh, I forgot, it bothers you to see me having a good time."

Chance and Roberta looked at each other. They knew this day had been too good to be true. Lately, it seemed that Lauren and Michael were always at each other, always waiting, always ready to throw down at the first hint of anything negative. It had been like that for over a year now.

"Come on, you guys, don't start," Roberta pleaded, stepping into the ice cold staring match.

"I'm not the one," Michael said matter of factly. "I'm just spending time with our closest friends, trying to have a little fun."

"Fuck you, Michael," Lauren interjected.

"Oh, now that would be a change of pace," Michael responded.

Immediately, Roberta whisked Lauren aside. It was time for some girl talk. Roberta knew that she and Lauren had grown somewhat distant over the last couple of years. In no way were they as close as they had been in their days at Howard University. Nor by any stretch of the imagination were they as close as Michael and Chance, who had spent much of their childhood together. But they were still close. Close enough for some girl talk, and besides, Roberta knew all too well how nasty these little spats could get. "Come on, girlfriend," Roberta said. "I gotta go pee again."

Although he hid it well under his cool exterior, Michael was seething. Chance knew it was best not to fan the fire, to allow the embers to cool on their own. He handed a twenty-dollar bill to the booth attendant and he and Michael began to toss cheerios into the ring. "Still no joy in paradise, huh?" Chance couldn't help but ask.

"War is hell," Michael said with a sad smile. "Marriage is worse." They tossed a few more rings. "Besides, we can only have one perfect couple in this little group. It's the yin and yang of life, know what I mean?" The two of them shared a smile. A smile that went back more than fifteen years.

Chance and Michael had first met at a Big Brothers' camp when they were both thirteen years old. Men who were stable, and often well-to-do, came up to these camps for a few weeks in the summer, hoping to inspire young, fatherless boys, to give them direction and strength, and build some sense of character. Chance and Michael had hit it off right from the start. Michael's father had died when Michael was very young. He had heard that his father was a good man and a hard worker, but had only cloudy memories of a few good times and a lot of lonely nights. Chance, on the other hand, had never known his father. Never heard stories. Never known his name. He chose to pretend the man was dead and that seemed good enough for him. At any rate, neither Michael nor Chance felt they needed any "part-time fantasy dad" and were perfectly happy spending the rest of camp talking to each other and playing endless games of one-on-one.

When the women returned, they found Michael and Chance still playing the ring toss game. The air was thinner now. The storm had passed. Roberta tugged Lauren to the booth, and the two of them grabbed the rings from the guys and began tossing the disks aimlessly into the booth.

"Whadda ya think you're doing?" Michael objected. "You're throwing off our rhythm!"

"What rhythm?" Roberta said smiling back at them. "You two are the only brothers I know who don't have any rhythm."

"And what's that supposed to mean?" Chance asked.

"Oh, don't get me started," she warned. "You know the two of y'all been doing the same dance since we met."

"And there's a problem with that?" Michael asked.

"Yeah, I can sum it up in three words," Roberta teased. "Pit-ti-ful!" Roberta answered with a jab as she and Lauren walked off arm and arm.

Michael gave Chance a "check your woman" look. After all, fellas can't let their women just run over them like that. But Chance smiled at the thought of Roberta and Lauren having a good time again. He really enjoyed seeing his beautiful wife happy.

"At least someone wants to keep his wife happy," Lauren said, noticing Chance's warm smile. "I think it's sweet."

"If you ask me, I think it's sad," Michael teased. "The man is obviously trying to get into her pants."

Roberta turned and walked back to Michael. She was doing that head thing that only black women with plenty of attitude can do. "And who asked ya?" Roberta quipped and then stuck out her sizable waist. "Besides, it's obvious that the man has already been in my pants." Score another one for Roberta. Michael was no match for her tonight. Roberta and Lauren slapped palms and continued walking.

"Yeah, but he ain't been there for seven months!" Michael blurted out. He knew that last statement would get to Roberta. She wasn't the kind of woman who liked her business in the street. And the fact that Chance had been discussing their love life, or lack thereof, with his best friend would bother her for the rest of the night.

Chance and Michael started off after their wives. The jolly young booth attendant, who was a light snack short of 300 pounds, leaped across the counter and brushed past Michael and Chance in pursuit of Roberta and Lauren. For such a big guy, the attendant was extremely light on his toes. In a dash, he was standing next to the women and handing them a large, velvety, cocoa brown stuffed monkey.

"What's this?" Roberta asked.

The booth attendant shook his head sadly. Some people just didn't get it, he thought, and these two must not be big fans of the Discovery Channel. "It's a very large stuffed monkey," the attendant responded with a deadpan face. "But if I were you, I'd watch out for the dust. I don't think anybody's ever won one of these things before. They've been hanging up in that booth for at least a year."

True, the monkey was a little dusty, but Roberta embraced it and held it close to her face anyway. She smiled a radiant smile that could have lit up the night. Michael and Chance joined them. Chance lost himself in a loving gaze between him and Roberta, watching her clutch the monkey to her motherly bosom.

"Ya know something, Chance?" Michael said suddenly as if he had just been presented with some great knowledge and, in his graciousness, was going to share it with Chance.

"No, what?" Chance asked, still not able to take his eyes off Roberta and thinking how loving she looked holding on to the adorable velvety soft chimpanzee.

"Now you know what your kid is gonna look like!" Michael spat out, along with a chest full of laughter.

"Why, I oughtta..." Roberta started as she raised the monkey above her head and threatened to bring it down on Michael's wavy crown. She stopped suddenly and grabbed hold of her stomach. "Oh my God," she whispered through tight lips.

"What is it, sweetheart?" Chance was almost afraid to ask. "Are you okay?"

Tears of joy started to well in her eyes. Cresting on her lashes, refusing to fall down her face. "The baby just kicked me!" she announced.

They all swarmed around her, each placing a gentle palm on her belly. This was a good moment. A special moment. Four people, the best of friends, all reaching out together to feel a tiny flutter of life. An incredible moment.

"That's my boooyyy!" Chance bellowed proudly, embracing his wife.

Michael and Lauren's eyes locked briefly, then Lauren's eyes quickly shifted away. Arms around each other, the four of them headed toward the park exit. It had been a long day, but all and all, it had been a good day. Chance had thought it was a crazy idea when Roberta insisted on them going to the amusement park. She couldn't go to an amusement park in her condition. But the doctors had said that the walking would do her some good as long as she was sensible and took it easy. When Michael rang the buzzer that morning, Chance had almost said, "No, we're not going. We've changed our minds. We're going to stay right here and work on the baby's room. Besides, Roberta wants to finish her book." But he didn't. He just grabbed their coats and helped Roberta out the door and into Michael's brand-new, fully-loaded Land Rover. Now he thought, about all the fun they would have missed. A nice warm day and a cool starlit night. It had been a good day spent with good friends.

"I've got one last request," Michael stated grandly, knowing that everyone would to ask him what it was. "I say we should ride one last ride together. Something slow, considering Roberta's condition, but at least one ride all together."

"Oh, I don't think so," Roberta sighed. "It's late."

"It was your idea to come here in the first place," Michael reminded her. "And you haven't been on anything, unless you count the port-a-potties. Come on, just one ride..." Michael dazzled her with that charming smile of his and that soft, cooing voice. It was that combination that had originally gotten him over with Lauren. Michael had a way of charming the skin off a snake. All he had to do was flash that smile.

"You'd better do it, Roberta," Lauren insisted. "You know how Michael gets when he doesn't get his way." It was a little stab but one she needed to make.

"Oh all right," Roberta said, finally giving in. "But I get to pick anything I want, right?"

Four

The nagging *umm-paa-paa* sound had filled her ears all day. Roberta had loved Ferris wheels ever since she was a child, and it was the only thing about them she found annoying. Other than that, she loved the feeling of slowly going higher and higher until you could see to the end of the horizon making her shudder with delight. As she got older, she compared the exhilarating feeling of looking beyond the dirt and soot of the city to where the air was clean, to the take off of a jetliner lifting up from the runway. Michael didn't share the same excitement about Ferris wheels. He stood on the loading platform shaking his head in disbelief as he watched the old, methodical wheel spin slowly.

"Oh, now this is a way to end an evening," Michael quipped sarcastically.

"You said she could pick anything she wanted," Lauren reminded him.

"But it's a Ferris wheel for Christ sake," Michael complained. "It doesn't do anything. It just goes around, and around and around. I mean, what kind of simple-minded fool came up with this concept?

It's a damn people mover for people who ain't going nowhere."

Michael did have a point, but the Ferris wheel's dullness made it a staple of every amusement park and carnival in the world. The design is simple: cranks and pulleys, powerful arms that grab hold of gondola-like cars and lift them up and over the loading platform, a simple wheel and pulley design that takes over and cranks the gigantic contraption in a revolving circle. Constant motion. Around and around. Michael felt as if he would be sick as he climbed from the loading platform into the rusted old bucket of the Ferris wheel's car. His eyes met those of the carney ride operator. Michael couldn't help frowning. The carney looked as though he hadn't seen hide nor hair of soap in years. He spit out a huge wad of tobacco. The slick, slimy black goo landed solidly on a nearby anthill, drowning the twenty or so ants carrying home a leaf for the queen's dinner. *Guess the queen will have to go without her tossed salad tonight,* Michael thought.

Lauren climbed into the seat next to him. A gentle breeze tugged at the nape of her blouse, pulling it gently away from her body and giving a glimpse of her soft, curvaceous breast underneath the fabric. Chance noticed immediately that she wasn't wearing a bra. The sight put him in a trance, and no matter how hard he tried, he couldn't turn his eyes away. The carney paid little attention to the sight, if he noticed at all. He simply lowered the thin metal bar across Michael and Lauren's waists and let the latch fall into place. The lock protruding from the bar fell into its catch and closed with a sharp snap. The carney didn't double-check the lock; there was no need, he'd been handling the Ferris wheel ride for over twenty years. He knew the machine like the back of his hand.

He shoved a large lever forward with his grimy hand, and the car holding Michael and Lauren began to glide back, giving way to another empty gondola to take its place on the loading platform.

Chance gestured for Roberta to go first. Her ice-cold stare sent a chill up his spine.

"Why didn't you just take a picture?" Roberta asked as she climbed into the bright red gondola. "You seemed to like what you saw."

Chance joined her in the Ferris wheel car. The cold metal of the ride's weather worn seat was warm compared to the frosty glare coming from Roberta's eyes. He thought of a thousand and one ways to deny her charges, but opted to say nothing. The carney flipped the thin metal bar over their laps. The latch landed with a dull thud against the catch. The sound was odd compared to the snap of the bar on Michael and Lauren's car. Again, the carney paid it no attention. No one noticed the hard, black leather strap of Chance's camera caught under the latch, disabling the sharp snap of safety. The carney pulled the massive lever in front of him. The gears ratcheted with an awful noise that sounded like ten huge Mack trucks stripping their gears at the same time. When they locked into place, the giant wheel began to revolve slowly in its ordained circular motion.

The wheel spun clockwise, and the car holding Chance and Roberta was now swinging above that of Michael and Lauren's. Michael leaned back as far as he could, looking up at Chance and Roberta. His weight caused the gondola to tip backwards.

"You guys all right up there?" he yelled.

Lauren grabbed him by the collar, snatching him upright into his seat. "You're not supposed to do that," she reminded him. "Didn't the man say not to rock the car?"

"How else are we supposed to have fun on this thing?"

The giant wheel continued to lift them higher into the air. Their bright yellow gondola swayed gently like a cradle. *Rock-a-bye baby on the tree top...*

"Besides, I wasn't rocking the thing," Michael added. "If I was rocking it, I'd be doing this." He leaned back and forth in the small car. The car rocked wildly as it climbed higher and higher.

"Don't be such an asshole, Michael," Lauren screamed. "Stop it!" Lauren had always had a thing about heights, but thought she had gotten over it. Right now, there was no doubt in her mind that the height thing was alive and well.

"Hey, take it easy down there, dog," Chance called from overhead. "You're shaking up the whole damn ride."

Chance was right. Michael's playful rocking started to cause the entire Ferris wheel to shake dangerously. The small grease-stained, red-and-white-striped box Lauren had been   clenching in her trembling hands was spilling its contents and showering the carney on the platform with stale salty popcorn. He picked up a few kernels and popped them into his mouth.

"Come on, man, ya sound like a little bitch up there," Michael shouted. "Rock the damn thing!"

Chance looked over at Roberta. He couldn't allow his best friend to dog him out like that. It was a guy thing, and Roberta was just going to have to understand. Besides, he wasn't going to rock the car a lot. Just a little tip back and forth to prove to Michael that he wasn't afraid.

As the small red car reached the crest, Roberta looked out over the city. Glimmering lights melted into the backdrop of twinkling stars. It was all so beautiful. So peaceful. The grace filling her eyes almost erased the annoying "umm-paa-paas." She didn't even notice the gentle swaying from Chance leaning back and forth inside the car. She turned to him. They shared a smile, and then Chance pushed against the thin metal safety bar.

The bar made a whooshing sound as it flew open. Chance's face went white instantly as he lost his balance. While his body fell forward, his arms flailed wildly, grabbing the cold, thin bar. He clutched it tightly, his feet dangling in emptiness. He watched his brand new camera land on the asphalt below and shatter into a million tiny fragments. Roberta screamed, clutching the side of the gondola. She reached out with one hand in a feeble attempt to give Chance something to hold onto. The gondola pitched forward, nearly throwing her out.

"Sit back!" Chance demanded. "I'm okay, just sit back."

Lauren sat, horrified in the car below. She wanted to scream, but nothing would come out. Michael tried to stand in the seat and reach for Chance, but Chance was just out of reach.

"Take it easy, man," Michael urged, trying to use his most reassuring tone. "We're gonna get you down." He could see the beads of sweat starting to sprout on Chance's face, his trembling arms struggling to hold on. "Anyway, didn't the man say not to get out of the car until the ride was over?" Michael tried to offer a reassuring smile.

"You mean this ain't part of the ride?" Chance let out a nervous chuckle. It was their way of saying that everything was going to be okay. If they could laugh about it and share a joke, then it was going to have to turn out fine. Wasn't it?

The carney worked the gears feverishly, attempting to get the Ferris wheel to move, but the whole mechanism had jammed. The undistributed weight put too much pressure on the mainshaft, and he could not get the lever to release. The veins in his head bulged, turning his face beet red. His grease-covered arms strained against the lever, but it wouldn't move.

"We'll be down in a minute," Michael assured Chance. "You okay?"

Chance tried to put on his most confident voice. "Yeah, man," he responded. "I'm fine."

"On a stack?"

This got Chance's attention. It was a call to truth. A saying from way back when. Time to put your cards on the table, look each other in the eye and come clean. "On a stack?" Chance replied. "I'm scared shitless."

Their eyes met. In that look you could easily see the love these two friends felt for one another. A look that only real brothers who have fought through life back to back and have come out still standing together could share.

Roberta continued to clutch tightly to the side of the gondola. The sharp edges of the rusted metal started to cut through her fingertips. She didn't know if she could hold on much longer. The slight flutter in her abdomen reminded her that she had to. She grasped the metal more tightly. A trail of blood started to trickle from her palms and down the length of her arms. *We've waited too long for this,* she thought. *I can't let go now.*

The lever snapped loose with a resounding "POP." The wheel jerked into motion all at once. The sudden jolt caught Roberta completely off guard, jolting her back and forcing the sharp metal deeper into the palms of her hands. Blood gushed out of the open wounds like a fountain. A thousand razor-sharp needles stung the palms of her hands. She let go of the stinging metal, even before she realized what she was doing.

"Roberta, no!" Chance screamed.

It was too late. In a flash, Roberta flipped out of the gondola and fell in a helpless, screaming blur through the air. She hit the railings, snapping her spine and flopping her down onto the loading platform like a rag doll.

"No!" Chance screamed. "Get me down from here!"

The wheel continued to lower slowly. Michael held Lauren close, hiding her face from the horror. Chance struggled, still suspended thirty feet in the air. The wheel wouldn't move fast enough. He looked down at the mangled, bloody heap laid out on the platform below, closed his eyes and let go of the safety bar.

Although his body sped down like a bullet, he felt as though he was falling in slow motion. He could see Roberta sprawled beneath him, his camera spread out in fragments. He tried as hard as he could to speed up the fall, but in his mind, his body continued to float down slowly like a feather gliding along in a gentle breeze. The loading platform resounded with a mighty crash when Chance hit the unyielding steel. Pain shot through his leg and set off alarms through his entire body. He could feel the bones in his right leg shattering beneath the skin. He wanted to cry out, but the only words that came to his lips were, "Roberta, hold on!" His eyes landed briefly on the carney's face. The old man stared blankly at Roberta's body sprawled out on the cold metal. A trickle of blood leaked from the corner of her mouth. Her eyes were open and wide, looking at nothing in particular. It was a sight he had never seen in all his years on this platform.

Chance rushed to Roberta, scooped her lifeless body into his arms and held her close. "Oh God please.." His eyes searched the heavens. "Please don't do this. Don't take them away from me."

Five

"**F**lat line, Doctor!" the young nurse repeated.

Dr. Wysse glanced up at the monitor and stared at the thin, green, unwavering line. The shrill pitch emanating from the machine registering life's end seemed to bounce off the walls and echo throughout the small room.

"Clear!" Dr. Wysse yelled, placing the lubricated paddles firmly on Roberta's chest.

Chance watched Roberta's stomach rise into the air as her body seized from the electrical charge. *Coming to you live, with seven hundred and fifty watts of uninterrupted power,* Chance heard a voice echo in the back of his head as the doctor increased the voltage on the machine.

"Clear!" the doctor repeated.

With each yell, everyone backed away from Roberta's body, each of them made sure they were nowhere near contact when the harsh jolts exploded out of the paddles and pulsated through Roberta's delicate frame. *How strange,* Chance thought, *this energy, this life force. Why is it that everyone else around the table seems so afraid of its power, yet they have no problem sending its seething force into the body of my dear sweet wife?*

"Clear!" Dr. Wysse screamed once more.

Chance moved in closer. There was nothing to fear anymore. No reason to stay clear. It didn't take the array of monitors overhead, wailing in unison and displaying that same unwavering green line, to make him understand what was happening. It wouldn't take one of the army of assistants that now stood around helplessly staring down, up, or anywhere else to avoid Chance's eyes.

And it didn't take Dr. Wysse's official words, which came in a less than audible voice. "I can't get her back," she said softly. A flash of the quiet, empty halls that had existed just moments before this heterogeneous group arrived entered her mind. She longed for that quiet once more. She wished she had never sulked about this being a dull and uneventful shift. She wondered again if her husband had tucked their son in for the night.

"Doctor?" the young nurse called Dr. Wysse's attention to one of the monitors. Under the high pitched wail of Roberta's heart monitor was another faint sound, a very weak, but noticeable beep...beep...beep.

"Get that preemie kit over here now!" Dr. Wysse commanded.

For the first moment in what seemed like an eternity, there was hope in this room. The faint beeping from the fetal heart monitor kept track of the tiny life inside Roberta's womb. Roberta was gone, but she had somehow held on to life long enough to deliver her unborn child into the right hands. Capable hands that could rescue the delicate being and bring it into a bright and wonderful world.

"Roberta?" Chance said with a bleak, cracking sound in his voice. Somehow he knew that she would never answer this call again. She would never again say, "What is it, dear?" or "In a minute, sweetheart." The tears poured down his face with no warning to their arrival and no hint of their end. Just an endless flood of tears.

"Someone please show Mr. Williams to a more comfortable area," Dr. Wysse insisted, not caring at this point if he realized that she wanted to get rid of him. "We'll come get him when everything is stable."

Chance was in a state of total disconnection. It took no effort for the lanky male attending nurse, tugging gently at Chance's arm, to pull him out of the door like a kite drifting in an errant wind. Chance stood outside the large double doors to Emergency Operating Trauma Room Seven. The sound of the swinging doors echoed in his head. *Frommp...frommp... froomp.*

The tiny scalpel started at the top of Roberta's abdomen. with the least bit of pressure, the razor-sharp tip pierced her skin. Even though she was dead, the amount of blood that came gushing out of her parting flesh was astonishing. Dr. Wysse stopped for a moment and looked at the one monitor that still beeped faintly underneath the wail of the failed heart monitor. The screaming siren started to bore a hole in her head. "Can I please have some quiet in here?" Dr. Wysse demanded. "Someone turn that damn thing off! Please." As chief resident, she didn't need to add the extra "please," but under the circumstances, Dr. Wysse felt that any display of good manners was in the best interest of all parties concerned. A hand quickly shut off all the useless screaming monitors. The room sequentially fell silent, except for the sound of the neonatal machine. A single sound filled the room. A tiny beep...beep...beep.

The soft folds of Roberta's flesh pulled away easily. Dr. Wysse stuck her hands inside the opening and felt the warmth of the blood-covered organs. Her fingers searched inside the womb to retrieve the unborn child. The first thing she felt was the head.

Then the soft thin tissue and hard bone around the arm. She felt the tiny butt. *Soft as a baby's bottom,* she thought. Maneuvering her hands deeper, she got a firm grasp and gently tugged. *Not too hard,* her brain reminded her, a thought left over from Dr. Samuel's obstetrics class. Gently, she reached beneath the tiny frame and felt the flutter of life. *Hang in there little one,* she thought. *I've almost got you.*

The tiny life spilled out of Roberta's womb, in total contrast to her still and lifeless body. The tiny thing moved, reaching and struggling to grasp hold of life. Dr. Wysse held the wisp of a being in her hands. The sealed eyes and labored breathing alerted her right away. The delicate skin was so transparent that she could see the blood flowing though its veins underneath. She held the slight whisper of a child in her arms as she stood over Roberta's body and looked into the gaping hole of her abdomen. The tiny child trembled and shuddered as it struggled to take in its first and last breath. Then it was gone. The room was completely silent.

Michael searched his soul for any strength he had to offer. It was excruciating for him to watch his best friend pace back and forth, pausing briefly only to wipe away a painful tear. Chance winced in pain with every step. Michael was sure he had broken his leg and insisted he have someone look at it, but Chance refused. He wasn't going to leave the room until this was all over.

Chance and Michael exchanged a glance. Michael tried, again, to think of something to say. *It's gonna be alright,* he thought that would be the perfect sentiment, but nothing inside of him made him believe it was true. Roberta's face popped into his mind. Her smile. Her warm and caring face. He thought about the countless debates and arguments he and Roberta had gone to battle over. Grueling hours that always ended in an embrace and a sarcastic 'we'll just agree to disagree' attitude. He looked again at Chance, needing to hold him and tell him that everything would be fine, but he still couldn't move.

Dr. Wysse carefully entered the waiting area. The room was cold and dimly lit. Back issues of tattered magazines sat on Formica topped tables. It was the kind of room where people sat and waited for news, any news, from down the hall and beyond the operation room doors. It was the kind of room that reeked of sadness because most of the time, the news that came wasn't good news.

Chance felt Dr. Wysse's presence as she entered. He whipped around, his eyes locking with hers, searching desperately for some sign of hope, the relief *At least we were able to save your child* in the doctor's eyes. But the only thing he saw in her eyes was *I'm sorry*.

"I'm sorry." Dr. Wysse tried to sound as controlled as she could but wondered if her voice was starting to crack. "We tried to do everything we could for your wife."

"Oh God." Lauren sighed.

"And the baby?" Chance asked with limited hope.

"We lost them both," Dr. Wysse finished. "There was nothing more we could do. It was just too early."

Chance collapsed as if his soul had been ripped out. Lauren raced to him, swallowing him in her arms. She noticed the cold and lifeless look on his face. Michael looked at the two of them, searching for something to say, but somehow he knew no words could relieve any of the pain that now filled this tiny room. He turned away and came face to face with the thought he had been running from the entire night. Suddenly, he couldn't bring himself to look at his best friend, who sat in an emotional heap upon the floor. Suddenly, he no longer wanted to think of anything to say. Suddenly, he knew that it was all his fault.

Lauren reached up to wipe the tears from Chance's face, and was shocked to discover that there were none. He had cried himself out. He had arrived at the base of his soul where there is no more pain. The spot where people go when they have given up on everything. The place where torment is its only reward. This was hell—not burning flames and sinners writhing in agony—but a place where it could get no worse and all life's pain was thrust upon you at one time. This truly must be what hell was all about, Chance thought, seconds before the room went black.

Most of the pews were empty in the small, quaint church. The sun streamed through the stained glass, turning it to rays of amber and violet, casting streaks of color across the two glistening coffins. Yellow lilies, white carnations and sprays of baby's breath surrounded the two rose-tinted boxes. Chance stood over the casket staring down at Roberta. Her eyes were closed. Her skin was darker than its usual honey brown. She had on too much make-up and mascara. She never wore mascara, Chance thought. She wore her chiffon dress, the one she had gotten for Michael and Lauren's New Year's Eve party and then didn't get a chance to wear because she spent the night throwing up with morning sickness.

A small, rotund woman stood alone in the choir box and sang, filling the room with her voice. She had one of those voices that could reach inside you and touch your soul, making you jump out of your seat yelling, "Sang, sister, sang!" She sang one of those sad, soulful hymns about going up yonder, one of those songs that makes your lips quiver and all of a sudden you find you're standing in your own puddle of tears. The church became a stream of mournful sorrow.

The tears rolled freely down Chance's face and splashed on the flower-covered coffin. He stared at Roberta one last time. He couldn't help noticing that her face looked tense and hollow. She didn't look like she was sleeping at all. She was far more beautiful than this when she slept. Her eyelids were lighter as the spheres of life danced underneath in her sleep. Her mouth twitched to the right side in a slight smile from some hidden laughter. Her nostrils flared with the slight guttural rumble in the back of her throat. No, the woman in this box wasn't sleeping. She was dead. And the smaller box that sat near her side contained too much pain for Chance to bear. He glanced at the tiny coffin briefly, then turned and walked away to join Michael and Lauren.

After the service, Chance walked slowly through the old cemetery with Michael and Lauren at his side. His right leg was stiff and rigid, making him walk with an obvious limp. He supported most of the weight on that side with a uniquely carved cane that looked like something Moses would have carried. A light mist had fallen, turning the rows of massive, gray concrete headstones a shade darker, and giving them the murky smell of a buried past. A slight breeze embraced him in a ghostly whisper as he glanced back briefly to the gentle knoll where Roberta and their child were laid to rest.

"It was a beautiful ceremony," Lauren said, mostly out of a need to break the cold silence.

"It was," Chance agreed. "And I want to thank you guys for all your help and support in getting through this."

"Hey, man," Michael started, in a what else are friends for? tone.

"No really, I couldn't have made it through this without the two of you. And thanks for letting me hang at your place for the past few days. I couldn't stand being at home alone."

"Our house is always open for you, man," Michael said. "You stay as long as you want."

Chance looked deeply into the eyes of his dearest friends. "You know, she wanted to name the baby after the two of you—Loren Michael." A reflective smile passed over his face. Michael and Lauren stopped dead in their tracks as Chance continued walking past the rows of large headstones.

The sun started breaking through the dark clouds as the three of them climbed into the back of the waiting limousine. Chance stared at Lauren's delicate face. Her large, round eyes filled once again with salty liquid. Chance reached out and wiped a tear away just before it ran down her face. Michael glanced over at the two of them. He felt a powerful urge to embrace Chance and say he was sorry over and over again. But he controlled the urge, turned away and quickly wiped away the tear trailing down his own face.

Chance stared out of the window as the limousine made its way through the small Virginia suburb. The streets were lined with large willows that hung so far out over each side that they met in the center, making it seem as if you were driving through a tunnel. Chance stared out of the window at each of the large, wood-framed, two-story houses with perfectly manicured lawns. They passed a small white house with a white picket fence. He and Roberta had passed that house many times on their way to Michael and Lauren's. Roberta had always commented that it was her favorite house on the block, even though it was smaller and less stately than the others. Chance stared at the large wicker swing on the front porch. A perfect seat for a young family on a warm summer night. A ghostly image began to appear on the swing. A woman and a handsome little boy sitting next to her. They were both dressed in bright white, giving them an angelic glow. Chance blinked his eyes several times trying to focus on the images, but he couldn't make them clearer, nor could he make them go away. He was just about to ask the driver to stop when the limousine screeched to a sudden halt, sending the three passengers in the back seat crashing to the floor.

"My God, what happened?" Lauren asked.

"Sorry," the driver announced as he lowered the dark, tinted dividing glass. "Had a kid jump out in front of me."

Chance climbed back into his seat and stared out of the front window. There he saw a small boy, perhaps five or six years old, trying to right himself from a fallen bicycle. Chance's eyes met the young boy's. There was something familiar about these eyes. Something that reminded him of Roberta. Suddenly he remembered the images on the front porch. His eyes darted back to the small house with the white picket fence, but the front porch was empty. The specters were gone. A young man, evidently the boy's father, rushed out into the street, retrieving the bike and the boy. The boy continued to stare into Chance's eyes even long after the father had pulled him back to their front yard.

The driver pushed the button to raise the tinted partition once again. The glass sealed against the rubber with a slight squishing sound, and Chance found himself staring at his own reflection. Staring into his own sad, empty eyes.

The limousine pulled past two flagstone pillars and into the driveway of Michael and Lauren's house. The long horseshoe drive was lined with trees and shrubs that led to the huge rustic home. The house was painted in earthy browns and taupes. Gentle swipes of cream and white graced the windows. Massive wood pilings supported a wooden bridge leading to a large flagstone porch. Huge double doors with brightly polished brass knobs and oval panes of etched glass stood majestically at the entryway.

"Michael, it's beautiful," Lauren had said the first time she had ever seen the house. "It's your best work yet!"

Michael had been designing this home for over a year when he got word that the prospective clients were trying to back out of the deal. He had put his heart and soul into every square inch of this house, adding everything he and Lauren had ever wanted in a home. The perfect kitchen with the gray marble-topped-cook isle in the center and the surrounding twenty-seven cabinets made of polished oak. The massive game room with the built-in 50" plasma-screen television and Dolby surround-sound speakers throughout. It was their dream home, and he had designed it for someone else. Now it looked as if this perfect home would remain empty.

Michael and Lauren thought long and hard before making an offer on the house. They knew the price was well out of their league, but it was the house they had always wanted. They made an offer and, with the help of Michael's company, they were closing escrow in a short twenty-eight days.

Michael opened the front door as Lauren escorted Chance inside. He leaned his weight on the sturdy staff as he walked across the slick marble floor. The open grand foyer gave way to a view of the upstairs landing and a large bay window that filled the room with bright sunlight. Lauren and Chance made their way up the stairs. Michael followed silently behind. Chance's fingers glided over the glossy white bleached wood of the banister.

At the top of the stairs, Lauren rushed ahead to a small table on the landing. The long wooden antique table was laden with photos displayed in bright, polished frames. Her hand went quickly to a picture of herself, Michael, Chance and Roberta. They were all smiling brightly on a warm and sunny day and holding a banner across their chests that read "The Best of Friends." Lauren laid the picture face down. The glass hit the table with a snap.

"I'm sorry," she apologized. "I meant to move that out of here before—"

"Don't," Chance insisted, lifting the photograph and staring at the images. "It's okay to think about her. It's even okay to say her name. She'll always be a part of our lives, and we shouldn't try to erase that." He put the photo back in its spot and then turned back to his friends. "And if we're going to get through this, you've got to stop acting like I'm some kind of emotional basket case. I'm a mature and rational adult, and I insist on being treated like one." Chance gave them a stern smile. "Now, stop treating me like an infant, okay?"

Lauren and Michael agreed with a nod. The three of them shared an embrace that gave them a moment of strength and hope.

"Now help me off with my clothes so I can go make pee pee," Chance added with a pouting child-like look on his face.

It took a moment before the joke could register with Lauren and Michael. They weren't sure if Chance's attempt at humor was genuine or an outpouring of bitterness towards a statement that he would never hear from his own child. Lauren and Michael both looked to Chance and upon seeing the smile taking over his face, they all broke down and laughed. It was a deep laugh that came from somewhere far beneath the pain, buried under the sorrow. It was a laugh that they all truly needed.

Six

L auren stood alone in the kitchen. Her hands were busy with the chore of chopping vegetables, but her mind was nowhere in the room. She thought about her friend Roberta and how she and Chance seemed to have the perfect marriage. She remembered the gentle kisses they shared so openly in public. She wondered how long it had been since she and Michael had kissed. A real kiss, with wet, parted lips and tongues dancing in rhythmic pleasure. She thought back to the last time she had kissed with that sort of passion. The sharp tip of the butcher knife demanded her attention with a quick prick of her index finger. She dropped the knife and pressed the bleeding finger to her lips.

"You all right?" Michael's voice called from behind her.

Startled, Lauren whipped around to find Michael standing in the doorway. *How long has he been standing there?* "Yes," she blurted out, not wanting to take too long to answer him. "I'm fine. How's Chance doing?"

"I guess he's putting up a good enough front for most people."

"Why do you say he's putting up a front?" Lauren asked, trying to clear her mind from previous thoughts.

"He's trying to act like his life can just go on," Michael said as he picked up a nearby napkin from a glass napkin holder and handed it to Lauren. "We both know that Roberta was all he had."

"Maybe he's stronger than you think," Lauren answered, wrapping the napkin around her bleeding finger.

"And maybe you know him better than I do." There was a curious tone in Michael's voice, one that suggested a hidden meaning.

"I'm just trying to be supportive." The definite period at the end of her words suggested there need be nothing else said. Yet she knew there would be more to come. Lots more. She and Michael had been at it so much lately that she felt a constant need to keep her guard up. It was like cats and dogs. Water and oil. Tyson and Holyfield. And there was never any warning when the rounds were about to start.

"I'm sure he appreciates that," Michael said sarcastically. "He loved her, and they really wanted that kid. It was something they both wanted." It was just a jab, but it was delivered with such a snap that the pain was numbing. Lauren sighed and closed her eyes, searching her mind for a way to escape the inevitable attack. "I gotta go to the office," Michael continued.

"I thought you were taking a few days off," Lauren said, taking the bait and pulling herself into the battlefield.

"I just decided to work half days." Michael turned his back to her and started toward the door.

"Half days?" Lauren's voice cracked. "Then why the hell am I taking off? I thought we were doing this together."

"Relax, I'll do my part." Michael turned with an "I got in the last word" attitude and headed out the door.

Lauren stormed through the door behind him, her eyes turning into narrow slats and her teeth clenched together. "You are so screwed up, Michael. Your best friend just lost his wife and baby."

"Really?" Michael turned back to her, ready for battle. "Well,

I guess I can relate to that, huh?"

"Don't start, Michael."

"Start what?" he feigned a tone of innocence. "I just said I could relate. First you need space from our marriage, I guess you could count that as losing my wife. And of course there's the fact that you won't have my child."

"I've told you, I'm just not ready for kids right now."

"Then when?"

"In time, Michael. In time." Lauren's eyes begged for his patience and understanding, but she knew all too well how this conversation would end. It would become loud and heated. There would be name-calling, and the trusty old shovels would come out to dig up the past. The past was the last thing she wanted to deal with at this point. Not after all they had just been through.

"And I guess you're the only one who gets to decide when that time is," Michael said, not waiting for an answer. He turned, hopped into his Rover and sped away. Lauren couldn't help feeling relieved that no other harsh words had been exchanged. Things could have been worse. Things could have been as bad as the argument two years ago when they ended up packing their bags and going their separate ways. All the bitter truths came out then, truths that were used to hurt instead of heal. Daggers of truth. Lauren had sworn after that day never to be that honest or truthful with anyone again.

Chance heard them arguing right underneath his bedroom window. He tried to block out as much as he could, tried to pull the pillow over his head to muffle their angry voices. He even tried turning up the sound on the thirteen-inch Sony in his room. The small, scratchy speaker called out "Lucy, 'chew got some 'splain'n ta do." He turned his eyes toward the set. Lucy and Ricky always brought a smile to his face. If only life could have been as simple as their black-and-white existence. If only he and his friends could have been more like the Ricardos and the Mertzes. Maybe then Roberta would still be alive. Maybe then they would still be awaiting the time when his own little Ricky would play "Babbaloo."

A single tear crept from the corner of Chance's closed eye and ran down his face. His mind drifted off into darkness.

Roberta's body fell helplessly through that darkness. Chance reached out for her, his straining fingertips missing hers by inches. Bam! Her body slammed onto the cold steel of the loading platform. Chance rushed to her, held her in his arms. Her body felt limp and strange, as if she were filled completely with liquid, no bone whatsoever. The haunting sound of the Ferris wheel's music mingled with wild laughter. Chance glanced up and saw Michael sitting alone in the Ferris wheel. Pointing. Laughing. Chance glanced back down to his hands, now holding his tiny embryonic child, who wailed plaintively.

Chance realized he was dreaming, but couldn't pull himself out of the painful nightmare. A flash of himself standing over Roberta's closed coffin entered his mind. He could smell the sweet pungency of the flowers and feel the cold misty air surrounding him. The lid on the coffin started to open with a high-pitched squeak that sent spikes of pain to the base of his ears. Chance backed away from the casket, turned away from the sound. But he could not stop himself from looking at what was coming out of the casket. Something in the back of his mind prepared him for the vision of Roberta's rotting corpse, worms crawling out of her eye sockets and her decaying skin sliding from her face. He prepared himself so he wouldn't scream at the sight of his beloved wife now turned into some hideous ghoul like a creature straight out of night of the living dead. Something inside him wanted to see her, to hold her once more. Something inside him needed to touch her and to say

'I love you' once more. He turned and faced the coffin, and then, like an over-wound jack-in-the-box, Michael popped up from inside the casket and burst out with a cackle of demented laughter. Chance tried even harder to awaken, attempting to run away from the demons in his head. Michael's laughter turned shrill and metallic, the sound of a thousand bells ringing at once, the sharp shrill metallic sound of a-Telephone.

Chance's eyes opened and darted around the room. He was back in Michael and Lauren's house. He had found a way to escape the nightmare and come back to reality, the reality that was punctured by the shrill sound of the ringing telephone. He reached pensively for the receiver. There was silence on the other end of the line. "Hello," Chance finally uttered in a groggy voice.

"Chance?" Michael's voice drifted in over the receiver. "Are you all right? I didn't wake you, did I?"

"Naw, man, I'm all right," Chance replied. For some reason he felt angry at the voice on the other end of the phone. It had just been a wild and insane dream, but for some reason, he couldn't shake the feeling. "I'm cool... what's up?"

"Is Lauren around?"

"I don't know, I guess. You want me to get her?"

"Uh, no, that's all right. Just let her know I called and...." Michael's voice trailed off into deep thought. "Forget it, man, don't tell her anything. Whatever I say, she'll find something wrong with it. I'm so sick and tired of this shit, I swear."

"Sounds like you've got problems, man. Anything I can do to help?"

"Yeah, wrap your hands around her throat for me and just squeeze until you hear something pop." Michael snickered at his own demented joke.

"Sure..." Chance said with an eerie calm. "Considering all you've done for me, I guess that would be the least I could do."

Click. The phone went dead.

Michael sat in his posh eighteenth-floor office staring at the dead phone in his hand. *What is up with you Chance?* he thought. *He sounded so weird, almost morbid.* For a fleeting moment, Michael wondered if Chance could ever actually... "Naw," Michael said as he shrugged off the thought.

Lauren sat on the verandah staring out into the night. The sky was a backdrop of sparkling black velvet. She loved it out here. It was quiet, peaceful, no one around for miles. The complete darkness made the stars seem even more brilliant, and the cool breeze coming off of the lake made everything seem clean.

What had happened to her life, she thought? What had happened to the days of her incurably romantic Michael, who filled their first apartment with a sea of yellow roses and would hand her chilled goblets of bubbling champagne? What had happened to the feeling she used to get when he held her close and traced the edges of her face with his finger? Perhaps, it was her fault; it seemed like things had changed when work started to pick up for her. Her grueling schedule made it impossible for them to spend a romantic moment togerther. But no, she remembered,that wasn't right. The only reason she had started working so much was that Michael was gone all of the time. It wasn't at all unusual for him to stay at the office until three in the morning, and then, come tiptoeing into the house reeking of some unfamiliar scent and rushing to the shower. It was Michael who had screwed up, not her.

Lauren stamped out a cigarette in the already overflowing ashtray and then quickly reached for another. She glanced at the phone, which she had heard ringing just a few moments ago. I should have answered it, she thought, but fuck it, if Michael wanted to know what was going on there, then he should have just kept his ass at home. She drained the contents of a nearby wine glass and lit the cigarette between her lips.

She blew out a thick haze that hung in the air like a cloudy veil. Her chin hit her chest as she closed her eyes and pulled the old gray knitted shawl up around her shoulders. She was so preoccupied with her thoughts that she never heard the light footsteps or even notice the two hands snaking up behind her.

Chance's hands crept slowly toward the back of her neck. Outstretched fingers strained nervously at first, and then, suddenly, took a firm grasp around her neck. Lauren jumped and turned around all at once, coming face to face with the smiling Chance, who was now gently rubbing her shoulders.

"What the hell are you doing with that thing in your mouth?" he asked in a menacing tone.

"Jesus, you scared me!"

"I thought you quit."

"I did. I only do it when I want to get back at Michael. He hates it when I smoke."

"Interesting revenge. Only one problem though—Michael ain't even here."

They both shared an uncomfortable laugh while Chance hobbled around one of the deck chairs and took a seat.

"You okay?" she asked.

"I'm fine," he lied, looking into her sad eyes. "So, still no joy in paradise, huh?"

"Some wounds take time to heal." There was a tremble in her voice.

"And some scars never go away." His words cut right to the core. "I know this is uncomfortable for you. I probably shouldn't even be here."

"Don't be ridiculous, we're your best friends. Where else would you go?"

She didn't mean to put it so bluntly, but the words just came out. Of course Chance had no place else to go. He had no family to speak of. Detention centers and foster homes were all he had to remember of his bitter past. The last things he needed right now were more painful memories.

"I heard you and Michael fighting earlier," he admitted. "I can't help but feel like the distance between the two of you is somewhat my fault. After all, it was me who told you about the affair he was having."

"It was something I needed to know," she said sadly.

"But still, it didn't have to come from me. I never wanted to hurt you. I don't blame you for hating me."

"I don't hate you," Lauren responded distantly. "I hate what happened. I hate Michael for screwing around. I hate that sometimes we allow passion to make us forget our responsibilities. I hate the fact that we have to sit here and have this conversation when all we really should be concerned with is how much we miss Roberta. I hate the fact that we can never go back and fix the things that happened. That this guilt will always be around, and no one will ever know the truth—I just hate the whole situation."

Her words lingered on the air for awhile, until Chance captured her gaze.

"But you don't hate me?"

Lauren went into a deep thought. "Okay, you're right, maybe I do hate you," she admitted. "Which means that a part of me must hate myself."

She was suddenly lost in her own thoughts. Stuck in a dark and lonely place. Chance hesitated for a moment, then reached out and took her hand in his. He wondered if she would pull away. He was grateful that she didn't.

"You know what I've always liked about you?" he said gazing into her eyes. "You are always so concerned about everyone else.

Always willing to sacrifice your own feelings. We've always been so much alike in that way. And then look how things ended up. Michael and Roberta should have married each other, and then we—"

Her eyes pleaded with him not to go any further, but it was true. It was obvious whenever the four of them had gotten into any intense discussion that she and Chance had always seemed to agree in direct opposition to Michael and Roberta. Michael and Roberta were two of a kind, hard-working, dedicated to their careers first and families second. Always striving for material possessions and trying to prove themselves better than everyone else. In a nutshell, Lauren thought they were both pretty anal-retentive. She and Chance had their artistic souls, their creative juices that seemed to flow so smoothly whenever the two of them were together. There was also something else unspoken between her and Chance. An unbridled sexual energy hung in the air, and at times was so suffocating that the two of them literally choked on its power.

They had struggled with this feeling for years, denying its existence, laughing hysterically whenever Michael or Roberta suggested some deep and powerful connection between them. It was all just talk, just an uncomfortable thought, until...

Lauren did not want to take this stroll down this twisted memory lane. "Roberta really did look beautiful today," her words came out of nowhere. "At peace. I bet she's looking down on us right now."

Lauren slowly slipped her hand away from Chance's and sat back in her chair, putting a noticeable distance between them. Chance suddenly felt abandoned and emotionally naked. He stared at her as he felt his body start to tremble. He rocked back and forth in his chair and bit down on his lower lip, a nervous habit he had picked up as a child. His eyes drifted up toward the stars. The warm, dark taste of blood trickled from his lower lip into his mouth.

"Are you all right?" she asked.

Chance quickly licked his lip and turned to her. "I'm fine," he answered with a warm yet undeniably false smile.

Michael's office was an advertisement of self-proclaimed excellence. Photos of him standing with city officials and business moguls in front of impressive buildings that his imagination had conceived. Plaques and awards in wood and brass attesting to his brilliance lined the rich burnt-orange walls. He sat behind the massive, glistening cherry desk with gold tips on each corner. He added a few lines to the drawing he had come in to finish, for a beautiful, three-story home nestled on a hillside in Malibu. Ridiculous, Michael thought, his pen drawing aimlessly. Nothing he could come up with would make the house float when it fell into the ocean after one of those famous Malibu mudslides. He found himself staring at a photograph inside a black lacquer frame. His and Lauren's images smiled back at him, but for some reason it was hard to recognize this couple. They were young, happy. Not a care in the world. "Love and Happiness," the words of the old Al Green tune floated into Michael's head. "Somethin' that'll make ya do wrong, make you do right..." Damn if ol' Al didn't have a point there, he thought.

"It's getting late," a soft voice said. Michael glanced up toward the door and saw Janice, his very young and very attractive administrative assistant. "So, if you're okay with it, I'm gonna go on home now...okay?"

It came rushing back to him in a flash. The first day he had interviewed her, she was so determined and energetic. He remembered the way she called him "Sir" during the interview— he'd wondered how long it would take to break her of that and have her call him "Mr. Hubbs" or better yet, "Mike." He remem- bered the long hours and grueling projects she endured with a smile and a gentle touch on his shoulder. He remembered that one night when they had worked a little too late, and he had gotten a little too close. He had walked her to her car, and as they had stood in the empty parking lot, their lips had come dangerously close. They had both backed off quickly and had never mentioned it since. But Michael still couldn't help feeling like a cross between Clarence Thomas and Billy Clinton in their formative years.

"You know, home," Janice continued. "That place with the refrigerator and the bed, and when the phone rings it's actually for me. It's getting late, so I'm gonna go *home,* okay?"

"Yeah, of course," Michael responded. He really hadn't heard a word but had gotten the gist of what she was saying. "You gonna be all right, or do you need me to walk you to the car?" He tried to stop the words as they came out of his mouth, but it was too late.

"Naw, I'll be all right," she chimed, patting the side of her purse. "Somebody mess with me, I got a little sumpin' sumpin' for they ass." She headed for the door, stopped and gave her usual smile. "Goodnight," she said, and with that she was out the door.

She could still feel Michael's eyes on her butt as she headed toward the elevator. *Too bad he decided to get back with his wife,* she thought, *I could'a had his ass.*

Michael stared back at the photograph on his desk. Janice's smile was sweet, but it would never be as enchanting as Lauren's. And there was nothing on God's earth that could match the sparkle in those caramel eyes. All of a sudden, he needed to be at home. He started to leave, but decided to give it a few minutes more. He wanted to wait until Janice was safely in her car and out of the parking garage. There was no need to tempt fate.

Seven

The oversized Pirelli off-road tires of Michael's Land Rover chewed up the gravel as he came to a stop in the long horseshoe driveway in front of his home. He stared out at the house, which suddenly seemed huge and empty. Three levels, forty-two hundred square feet, five bedrooms, four baths, a rumpus room and a pool. It was all too much for two people. He and Lauren had once dreamed about filling this home with kids and family pets. The perfect home for the perfect family. Weekend barbecues by the pool with a few other parents from the PTA. Sleepovers and birthday parties on the weekends with little Ashley or Michael Jr. and his friends. It had all seemed so perfect, before life got in the way.

Yeah, Michael thought, *life's a bitch and then the woman you love turns into one.* He shook off the contemptuous feeling as quickly as it came. There was no reason for him to be upset with Lauren. He was the one who had screwed up. She was just reacting the way any normal, red-blooded, American, black woman would act. As a matter of fact, she was acting more civil than most. After all, she did take him back, and he had never once come home to find his car and clothes going up in a raging bonfire on the front lawn. They had agreed to forgive each other and try to pull their lives back together again. And that's just what he intended to do.

Michael walked slowly to the front door and slid his key into the slot of the gleaming brass lock. He started to turn the key and couldn't help thinking how quiet it was inside. Not a single light burning in any window. It wasn't that late, and besides, Lauren always left some light on when she was home alone. But she wasn't alone. Chance was there. After all that had happened today, Michael had completely forgotten about their house guest. Michael's mind quickly shot into rewind, replaying the conversation between him and Chance earlier that evening. "Anything I can do for you?" Chance had asked. "Just wrap your hands around her throat and squeeze a little," he had replied. "That's the least I can do after all you've done for me," Chance had said with that eerie tone in his voice, and then the phone had gone dead.

Jesus Christ, Michael thought, what if he actually did it! What if Chance had actually snapped and was trying to get back at him for Roberta's death. *The man just buried his wife and child this afternoon, and a few hours later I'm making stupid jokes about strangling my own wife.* Michael's mind reeled. How could he have been so heartless? An image of Lauren sprawled out on the cold marble of the foyer floor burst into his mind. Her bloodshot eyes bulged from their sockets, and there were black-and-blue pressure marks around her neck. Stunned, Michael forgot how to open the front door, turning the key and pressing the latch at the same time. He fumbled with the slippery hardware, cursing his hands for not moving fast enough.

The front door flew open quickly, and the cold, empty foyer greeted him with a haunting silence. His eyes darted from room to room. The empty hunter-green leather sofa faced him across the hall. The antique coffee table with the *Architectural Digest* magazines and brass lamp stood untouched. Michael walked pensively into the living room. His footsteps tapped on the glistening marble floor and echoed off the antique linen walls. "Lauren?" he whispered in a calm voice. There was no answer, but there was no sign of a struggle either. Nothing amiss, no blood, no dead wife, no 9-1-1. *You paranoid dumbass,* he thought to himself as he looked around the room. *The only one losing it here is you.*

He quickly made his way up the staircase, taking two steps at a time, slipped into the bedroom and took a seat at the edge of the bed. Lauren was there. Lying safe in her bed, fast asleep. At least she appeared to be sleeping. Her eyes were closed and her breathing was deep. Michael reached over and gently moved one of the long thin braids away from her face. She was beautiful. He leaned in close and inhaled deeply. He almost choked from the stench of the cigarette smoke. *I could even go for one of those about now,* he thought as he kissed her gently on the cheek.

"I left your dinner on the stove," Lauren announced with no trace of sleep in her voice. "You probably want to nuke it for a couple of minutes." She could feel Michael's eyes caressing her, his delicate index finger tracing the side of her cheek. He had amazingly soft hands for a man, she had always thought. Always well manicured and not much larger than hers.

"I'm sorry," he whispered. "I just had a lot on my mind and I needed to get away."

A lot on your mind? she thought. *What about the rest of us?* But she kept the words from escaping her lips. What would be the point of starting another argument? Besides, she could tell by his touch what he wanted. And it had been a while since they had done it. As a matter of fact, they hadn't even come close to anything since Roberta's... The thought hit her like a diesel, and suddenly she was no longer in the mood. She started to turn to Michael and tell him that she just wanted to be held, but it was too late. His pants were now around his knees and the small bulge inside his silk boxers was already starting to grow. Michael's hands pawed at her underwear, pulling them down around her thighs. He entered her. She closed her eyes, bit her lip and braced herself. She knew it wouldn't take too long, and very shortly they would be lying back to back and drifting into a sound sleep. In the meantime, neither one of them noticed the sliver of light coming through the bedroom door. And neither one of them realized that Chance was standing just outside the open door, watching.

Michael slammed his fist down on the steering wheel, causing the blaring horn to slice through the still afternoon air. "Come on, ya clowns," he shouted out of the driver's window. "Let's move it!" Traffic on I-95 was at a complete standstill, and it wasn't even rush hour. Orange cones shrunk the massive four-lane highway into one single lane ahead. "You'd think these dumb asses would work on the freeways when nobody is on 'em," Michael raged as he turned to Chance sitting in the passenger seat. "Like at one or two in the morning."

Chance made no attempt to respond, allowing Michael's burning road rage to smolder out. It wasn't the traffic that upset Michael; it was the fact that this was the first time he and Chance had been alone together since the accident. And now, here they were, stuck in traffic, forced into some sort of meaningless, idle "gotta be careful of what you talk about" conversation.

Michael searched his mind for something to say. Anything. He saw a light-blue '69 VW Beetle pulled off on the shoulder. The radiator spewed out a steady stream of white smoke. *Sitting still so long in traffic will overheat those tiny old engines every time.* He thought of punching Chance hard in the shoulder like when they were kids, and blurting out "Slug bug. No slug back!" But they hadn't played that game since elementary school, and besides, it had always ended up with somebody punching too hard and somebody else getting hurt. He remembered the time when his burly uncle Bill had to break up a fight between the two of them as they drove by the Autohouse VW dealer and ended up in a slugfest in the back seat of Bill's old Buick. His uncle had started yelling in that deep, gruff voice of his, "The next time anybody punches anybody, it's gonna be me. And one of you guys is gonna be very sorry." Michael knew it was an empty threat. His uncle had a mean bark, but his bite had been defanged years ago. But Chance's reaction to the booming voice was the clincher. Chance actually wet his pants and spent the rest of the ride trembling in the corner of the car, rocking back and forth and biting his lower lip.

"How ya holding up there, dog?" Michael finally asked, watching Chance stare aimlessly out of the window. "Your leg all right?"

"It only hurts when I walk," Chance replied distantly. "Riding doesn't bother me."

"Yeah, I know. I just thought, being cramped up in this car, you know." Michael's attempt at idle chatter was failing miserably.

"I'm all right, okay?" Chance reassured him. "Stop tripping."

They crept closer to the construction site. A powerful jackhammer-like machine mounted on the front of a truck slammed a huge metal blade into the asphalt like a guillotine. *Wham-wham*, over and over the mighty wedge drove into the street. Chance watched the machine, hypnotized. For some unknown reason, each blow reminded him of Roberta crashing to the ground.

"This traffic's a bitch," Michael sighed.

"And then you die," Chance muttered under his breath. They crept past the construction site as traffic eased up ahead. The pounding noise drifted off in the background, returning the interior of the car to complete silence. Chance closed his eyes and tried to erase the painful thoughts.

"I don't know what to say anymore, man," Michael said, a desperate search in his voice. "I keep playing the whole thing back over in my head, and wishing I had just kept my damn mouth shut. If I hadn't insisted we all take that last ride—"

"Let it go, man," Chance cut in. "We can't go back there. We can't change anything. Just let it go." Their eyes met. It was the first time since the hospital that Michael could remember looking into Chance's eyes. And there was love in those eyes, a love for a friendship that had been around since the beginning of time, a friendship that could withstand anything. "Besides, you're supposed to have my back today," Chance reminded him. "To help me get through this, remember? We're going through this together, like boyz, ya know what I'm saying."

They shared a smile, also the first in a while. The air was much lighter now. It was easier to breathe in deep gulps of forgiveness. Chance reached over and clicked on the radio. WHTZ was playing soulful oldies. Smokey crooned over the Alpine speakers...

"I'm just about at

The end of my rope

But I can't stop trying

I can't give up hope..."

"Ah, man, remember this one?" Chance shouted out, cranking up the volume a few decibels. "This was the jam!" Chance began to sing along with the soulful sound, egging Michael to join in. Michael's voice was harsh in comparison to his, and Chance slowly drifted back into silence. Michael continued singing at the top of his lungs, his voice cracking in the attempt to keep up with the smooth falsettos of Mr. Robinson and his Miracles.

Michael pulled off I-15 at the River View exit, the music still blaring in the car. He was lost in his own world and was letting the music soothe troubles away. If the car had been silent at this moment, he would have felt the icy cryptic glare directed toward him from the passenger seat. He would have also heard when the final ties of everlasting friendship snapped forever.

Chance walked slowly up the eight concrete steps that led to the front door of the town house. He stared at the polished brass doorknocker in the center of the door. The engraving on the brass read, "Welcome to Our Home." His hand reached for the large oval handle of the knocker. For a moment, he felt the urge to give the door just a light tap, praying that Roberta would come racing to open it. She would peek through the crescent-shaped beveled glass, fling the door open and take him in her arms, begging him to forgive her for playing such a terrible prank. But it wasn't a prank; it was all too real. And the cold wave of reality crashed over him like a tsunami over a tiny, deserted island.

"You okay with this?" Michael asked pensively, standing next to Chance at the front door. "'Cause, if not, I can run in and get whatever you need, and you can wait in the car." Michael had a point. Chance had only returned home once since the accident, and that experience had sent him on a high-speed ride straight to the edge of the Potomac River, where he had stood for hours contemplating taking his own life. He swore that night he would never go back inside that house. But Michael had insisted they come back to collect his things and to make arrangements to put the town house up for sale.

"I'm okay," Chance insisted, pulling out his key and starting for the lock.

"On a stack?" Michael asked.

Chance thought about it for awhile. "Yeah, on a stack." Chance turned the key, and the door glided open effortlessly, as if to welcome him back home. Dusty sunlight filtered through light cream chiffon curtains, giving the room a hazy, colorless glow. He stepped onto the thick Persian runner that covered the glistening hardwood floor. In the back of his mind he could hear Roberta's voice calling to him with her daily "No shoes, I just did the floor." Her house slippers still sat near the front door. Her presence was all around, filling every corner of the room and embracing him as he stepped through the door. He could feel her, smell her, sense her presence all around him and it hurt him badly not to be able to touch her. He needed at this very moment to hold her close and say, "My God, I miss you so much."

"This wasn't a good idea," Michael admitted as he wrapped a comforting arm around Chance's shoulder, guiding him out of the room. "Let's get out of here."

Chance had gone too far to turn back now. He pulled away from Michael with a sudden jerk and headed down the long hallway. Each step took him further into the past and deeper into despair. He stopped at a room halfway down the hall, a former study where Roberta had spent countless hours reading and studying for her exams. She had returned to college just a couple of years earlier, vowing to finish something she had started before she was too old and too tired. She had quit school during her senior year in an effort to support Chance's dream of becoming a renowned artist. They had spent thousands on photographic equipment, and it was up to someone to be the adult and take care of the bills. Roberta had taken on the responsibility with fervor, absorbing herself in the chore of paying the bills, taking on all the overtime and odd jobs she could get. She had been poor once before, and she never wanted to be poor again.

Now the room was empty, almost barren, with a carpet of brown paper covering the floor and cans of paint and used brushes that stuck in a plastic tray of dried pastel-blue paint. One wall was completed, the soft blue trimmed in a bright white.

Unused rolls of off-white wallpaper printed with blue bears holding pink and yellow balloons sat neatly in a corner of the room. A menagerie of stuffed animals waited on the floor of an open closet, animals that would never meet their intended master. Pools of pain began to crest in Chance's eyes.

"Man, don't do this to yourself," Michael begged, but Chance fought past him and continued down the long, dark hallway. He reached the room at the end of the hall, stepped inside and closed the door behind him.

Entering this room was like entering another world, a world that had been frozen in time. Nothing had changed. Everything was the way he and Roberta had left it the morning they had rushed out to join Michael and Lauren at the carnival. Their clothes were still scattered on the floor. The open packs of saltines and Oreos that started Roberta's every morning and ended her every night were still on the nightstand. A paperback novel entitled *The Rekindred Spirit* sat near the bed. He picked it up and stared at the woman in the long, flowing, white nightgown on the cover. A gentle breeze seemed to toss her auburn hair as she stood at the edge of a cliff. The caption under the title read, "Not even death could keep them apart." A business card Roberta had used as a bookmark fell from between the pages and floated to the floor. Chance stared at the cartoon of a baby wearing a surgical mask and holding a stethoscope drawn on the face of the card. Written near the drawing were the words, "We'll see you and your baby next Friday at noon."

Tears flowed so copiously that Chance didn't even bother to wipe them away. He picked up the rumpled pillow where Roberta had last laid her head. He held it close and inhaled deeply, catching the light, sweet scent. He closed his eyes to see her face and imagined stroking her soft brown cheek.

"You all right in there, man?" Michael's voice called out from the other side of the door. "I really think we should get out of here." It had been too soon. The accident, the hospital, the funeral. It had all gone by so fast that the three of them had been caught in the whirlwind, but standing here now, Michael knew all too well that the grief his best friend was going through was related to him. He knew that no matter how small a part he had played in the catastrophe, the outcome would always be the same. He had suggested they take that last ride, and now Roberta was dead.

The bedroom door flew open and released a blinding flash of light spilling from the bedroom window. Michael winced as the sudden brightness dilated his pupils. "You want to give me a minute here, you sonofabitch?" He heard Chance's angry voice cry out instants before a vise-like grip took hold of his collar.

The two men locked eyes and Michael could see plainly the pain and fury raging inside Chance.

"What's up with you, man?" Michael's shocked voice cracked. "Get off me."

Chance spun Michael around and slammed his back hard against the bedroom wall. Michael's instinct told him to ball up his fist and knock the crap out of Chance, but he held back. He had seen Chance like this a couple of times when they were younger, but he had never before been on the receiving end of his fury.

"Chill out, man!" Michael warned. "I'm just trying to talk to you."

"You want to talk?" Chance's voice hovered somewhere between a whisper and a madman's scream. "What do you want to talk about, Michael? You want to talk about my wife, my dead wife? Or do you want to talk about my dead son? Maybe you want to tell me how sorry you are and how it was all just a terrible accident."

Chance flung Michael across the room, making him stumble

and fall into the large oak dresser. The attached oval mirror teetered precariously for a moment and then crashed onto the hardwood floor. The glass shattered into sparkling fragments, cursing Michael for the next seven years.

"You want to talk, then talk!" Chance screamed. "But let me tell you something, Michael, it doesn't help. It doesn't take away the pain. And it definitely won't bring them back. So what the fuck is there to talk about?"

Tears started to well up in Michael's eyes. He couldn't believe what he was hearing. He couldn't believe that he was being blamed, cursed, by someone he cared so much about. He wanted so much to go to Chance and embrace him, to beg his forgiveness, but he knew he wasn't the only one to blame. It wasn't totally his fault.

"Goddammit, it wasn't my fault!" spilled out of Michael's muth before he could think.

There was a brief silence as the world stood still, and all familiar life seemed to stop. Suddenly, Chance lunged across the room, hitting Michael with all his weight. The two men hit the floor with a powerful thud that rattled the windows. Chance was livid. Possessed. He hit Michael with an endless succession of overhand blows that reached back somewhere into a dark childhood and ended with a mangled soul laid out on a cold steel platform. Michael's arms flailed helplessly in the air, trying to hold and embrace his friend, trying to reach out, grab him and say, "Hey, remember me? I'm the guy you grew up with. The guy who loves you. Your one and only true friend."

But Chance's vicious beating did not stop, and Michael's arms finally fell helplessly to the floor. Chance looked down at the unconscious mound of bloody flesh beneath him. "Go ahead, Michael," he said with an eerie calm. "You had something you wanted to say. Go ahead, talk to me."

The front door almost smacked Lauren in the face as it flew open while she was passing by. She dropped the handful of bills she'd just picked up along with the new issue of *Essence* on the marble floor. She was just about to light into Michael, who was charging through the front door, until she saw his face. Apparently someone else had beaten her to it. "What the hell happened to you?" she asked, reaching toward his bruised and battered face. She immediately assumed he and Chance had been in a car accident, or worse, in one of the car jackings that had recently been taking over the city. Maybe they had been mugged. Michael's face looked as if he had run into a cracked-out Mike Tyson in a back alley. She thought about checking his ear to see if it was all there, but she knew that would be in bad taste. "Are you guys okay?"

Michael pulled away sharply as Chance entered. Lauren was shocked to see that Chance didn't have a scratch on him. Neither man would allow their eyes to meet hers. Michael stormed up the stairs, and Chance leaned back against the wall, chewing on his bottom lip. Lauren didn't know where to start, but since it appeared that Chance hadn't even been at the scene of Michael's accident, she rushed up the stairs after her husband.

Lauren entered the master bathroom slowly. Her eyes met Michael's in the reflection of the bathroom mirror as he stood there examining the bruises on his face. "You want to tell me what happened?" she asked in her most caring voice.

Michael had resolved during the long, silent ride home not to talk about it. He was never again going to think about what had happened, and when Chance finally apologized, he would just say nonchalantly, "For what?" As far as he was concerned, the whole thing was better forgotten. Instead, the words, "The man's a fucking basket case." spewed out of his mouth.

"What man?" Lauren asked, truly confused.

"What man do you think?" There was venom in his voice. He was like a cobra ready to strike at anyone who passed.

"Chance hit you?"

"No, Chance beat the crap out of me, that's more like it." He knew as he said it that this incident was never going to be forgotten. Not in his mind. "He was fine one minute and then out of nowhere..."

"Something must have happened." She wanted to hear the whole story, not the one-sided "he hit me first" rendition this was starting to sound like. "He wouldn't have just snapped like that."

"You're always trying to find an excuse for him." He was hoped that for once she would just be on his side and not try to be the voice of reason. She hadn't known Chance as long as Michael had. She didn't know how distant he had become after his mother mysteriously disappeared, and was found dead weeks later, an apparent victim of "suicide." She didn't know about all the run-ins with the foster parents and the institutions that had claimed he was incorrigible and deeply disturbed. She didn't know what he was capable of. No one did, except Michael.

It had been back in college that Michael first saw the depths of Chance's soul. In the past, Chance had told him about some strange things, but Michael had never seen any violent displays first hand. They had been in the Langly study hall, which was more a senior hang out than a place to study. Someone always sneaked in a case of beer or had a joint or two to take a hit on. There was a pool table in the center of the room, and the music was always loud enough to seem to make the balls on the table move magically on their own. The back room was used occasionally, whenever there was a willing girl around, and rumors of the trains being pulled by the football team on an unsuspecting sophomore were not hard to believe.

Chance had come strutting into the hall with this hot little white chick on his arm. She was a knockout, one of those girls with long blonde hair and baby doll eyes. She had small, pouting lips that would all but disappear when Chance swallowed them in a wet kiss. And she had a butt that could rival any sister's. The whole room had stopped cold when they walked in. It wasn't because he had the nerve to stroll in with a white girl--after all, it was the eighties, and even in the South, the racial thing was pretty liberal. The clincher was that this chick was the ex-girlfriend of Hubert Medcalf, one of the meanest, most blockheaded, no-neck, shit-for-brains crackers you'd ever want to meet. And there he was, shooting pool with a few of his beer-guzzling buds.

Michael had tried to tell Chance to duck, but it was too late. The back end of a pool cue came crashing down across his back. The big white bull lifted Chance off his feet and tried to choke him with the rest of the cue stick until Chance nearly passed out. Chance lay on the floor gasping for breath as the bull slapped the girl around and kicked her out of the room. Campus security came in quickly and glossed the whole thing over. Michael sat on the floor next to Chance offering his support, but Chance's mind had slipped off somewhere else. He just sat on the floor rocking back and forth and biting his lower lip.

Late that night, the entire campus was filled with sirens and red flashing lights. Somehow, Medcalf had managed to lock himself in his dorm room, break off the door locks and handles on the inside, douse the room with ten gallons of gasoline and then set himself on fire. His bloodcurdling screams could be heard all the way back to Langly Hall, where Chance enjoyed a brew and gave Michael a bone-chilling smile.

Michael tried to forget that night as soon as it was over. But to this day, whenever he saw the old black-and-white classic *The Bad Seed* on late-night TV, with the scene when the bad-ass little girl burned up the janitor in the basement, he couldn't help remembering that night, and the way Chance had smiled.

"Let's just say you don't know him as well as you think." Michael finally said, running cold water over his bruises.

"Well, if he's all that bad," she countered, defending him again, "Then maybe we should get him some help."

"I think the man is beyond help," Michael snapped bitterly. "Besides, the problem is obvious. He thinks I'm responsible for the death of his wife and child."

"You can't believe that," Lauren insisted. "Chance doesn't believe that. He said so himself!"

"Look at my face, sweetheart. I think he's changed his mind."

"And what about you?" Lauren's voice desperately sought to resolve this. "What do you believe?"

"I know that my best friend's wife and child are dead," Michael sounded lost and empty. "It really doesn't matter what I believe anymore."

Eight

The law office of David Glick, Attorney at Law, was much too dark and had far too much mahogany lining its walls. The windows were extremely tall and slender, and even they were covered by wooden shutters that fought against the sunlight, allowing only small slivers of light to cut through the room. Chance sat in one of the oversized, comfortable-looking, yet much too firm, burgundy leather chairs. In the other chair beside him sat Lauren. She was obviously uncomfortable about being in the room with the two men, and nervously traced circles with her long, bright-red fingernails around the upholstery tacks in the chair. Even though she looked uneasy, Chance was glad she was there. The pending lawsuit against the carnival was proving to be more painful than anyone had anticipated. It was no one's fault and no one wanted to take the blame; the only thing everyone could agree on was that it had been a terrible accident and never should have happened.

"All things considered, I think we have an excellent offer," the attorney stated through a large, wiry moustache. Chance was amazed how much the man resembled a sea lion stuffed into an expensive suit. His face came to a narrow point, and he fidgeted constantly with the huge pile of manila folders on his desk. "We could still force them into court and perhaps get more, but we'd be looking at a pretty long trial."

"Why should he settle out of court? It was their fault." Lauren had shifted into her all-business mode. This was one of the traits Chance admired about her and the reason he had asked her to come along to the meeting. She was like a pit viper when it came to dealing with money, one of the necessary evils of going into business for oneself. "It sounds to me like they're playing on his emotions. Tragic accident, painful memories, that sort of thing."

"And it's for those kinds of reasons that I lean toward accepting their offer." The attorney spat out his words like machine gun fire. "Besides, it's their contention that it was your husband--Michael, isn't it?--and Chance who actually caused the accident in the first place, and not a mechanical malfunction at all."

"They're saying that I killed my own wife?" Chance's question came more out of anger than disbelief.

"Well you and I know that that's a bunch of crap," Glick said to calm Chance. "But they're going to introduce a few eyewitnesses, some engineering experts. They'll even try to clean up one or two of the carneys and bring them in as reputable, clean-cut carnival ride operators. You and I know that they're all a bunch of dope heads, and the accident happened because the asshole just wasn't paying attention, but they will use anything they can to basically draw this thing out and hope that you go away."

The words all came at Chance too fast and made him wonder if Glick ever paused to take a breath. The ride operator at the carnival hadn't looked like a dope head. Just an average, hard-working guy in desperate need of a bath. Chance was in no mood to relive the whole chain of events in an effort to point the finger at the man. If he would point the finger at anyone, it would be Michael, and if Michael was really to blame, then how many fingers did that leave pointing back to himself? *How can they say that I killed my own wife and child?* The question droned on in the back of his head.

"So what do you suggest?" Lauren asked. She couldn't wait any longer for Chance to come out of his daze. She had almost pulled one of the bright brass upholstery tacks out of the arm of the chair. "Should he take the offer or not?"

"Well, that's completely up to chance." Glick paused for a moment and chuckled to himself at the crude pun. He didn't mean completely up to "chance,"; he meant completely up to Chance. He held back the chuckle, passing off the tickle it gave him as a scratchy throat and faked a cough. "Whatever decision you make, we'll go with. I'm just saying that right now we have a good offer on the table, and it's worth considering."

All eyes turned to Chance, whose gaze was lost in the sliver of sunlight scratched across the floor.

Glick checked his watch while he tapped a beat on his desk with his black-lacquered Cross pen. The tapping started to sound like a paragraph in Morse code, or the annoying beat of the "Macarena." Lauren shot Glick a look that made the tapping stop instantly. "Why don't I leave the two of you alone for awhile so you can discuss this," he said, taking the hint, and quickly headed out of the room.

The large door closed with a whisper, leaving Chance and Lauren alone in the dark room. Chance's eyes shifted from the sliver of light on the floor to the light in Lauren's eyes. Another leak of light through the shutters hit her face and made her eyes sparkle honey-gold. She offered him a slight smile through dark, thick lips that gave way to glistening ivory. His eyes traced over her entire beautiful face but gave no clue of what was on his mind.

"It must be awfully cold and lonely in there," she said as she reached out and took his hand. Her hands were cool and soothing. Soft and smooth.

"It is," he answered, staring deeply into her eyes. "You should come in and keep me warm."

His words caught her a little off guard. "I think it's safer if you just join me out here in the real world." She gave his hand a light squeeze and a friendly pat, as if to put an end to that line of thought. "I know this is difficult, and nobody is expecting you to figure out the rest of your life right here and now. Whatever you decide is okay. Just tell me what you want to do."

Her voice was hypnotically soothing, leading Chance to a peaceful place. For the first time since that terrible night, he knew just what he wanted to do. He wanted to live. He wanted to stop hurting, to pick up what was left of his life and live. He wanted, if just for a moment, to stop thinking. "You know what I want to do?" he asked. There was a slight gleam in his eye, which made Lauren even more curious.

"Tell me," she said returning his eager glance.

"I want to get the hell out of this dungeon and go somewhere where people are having a good time."

That was all Lauren needed to hear. It was a positive note, like the first song of a robin in the morning after a night filled with rain. She grabbed her coat, stood and offered out her hand. Chance's eyes lingered for a moment on her long, shapely legs caressed in sheer black silk stockings. He took his cane in one hand and her hand in the other, and the two of them quickly exited the dark, dreary law office.

Glick was stuffing his face with a cream cheese bagel when he looked up and saw Chance and Lauren emerge from his office. He sprung to his feet and poked his pointed little face in their direction. "What's up?" he asked. Bits of bagel sprayed from his mouth as he spoke. "Everything all right?" Glick quickly tried to wipe the smeared cream cheese from his wiry moustache and put on his most astute counselor's face.

"Everything's fine," Chance said with a broad smile. "I'll call you in a few days." Chance and Lauren continued through the lobby, trying to hold back the laughter that leaked out in snickers and smirks. David Glick was a funny-looking man anyway, and now looked like a seal with cream cheese smeared all over his face.

Michael slammed the phone down on the receiver seconds after the annoying click of the ring switched over to voice mail. It was the third time he had called the house, and he couldn't stand to hear his own recorded voice again. At first he was just curious to find out what had happened at the attorney's office, but now he was downright pissed at Lauren for not calling and being nowhere to be found. It reminded him of the night two years before when he and Lauren had broken up.

Lauren had called in the late afternoon and left an alarming message, "Fuck you, Michael, and that bitch you're fucking." Short, sweet and to the point. The empty click that followed dropped a heavy weight into the pit of Michael's stomach. *What does she know? How does she know?* A thousand and one questions flooded his mind. His first instinct was to rush home and tell Lauren how wrong she was, to try somehow to convince her that it was all a big mistake. But unless he knew how much she knew, the plan seemed severely flawed. He decided to pick up the phone and give her a call. She wasn't in her office and she wasn't at home. Sweat started leaking out of him in places he never knew possible.

Lauren had stayed out all that night and hadn't come in until late the next day. He'd held back the burning urge to ask her where she had been. It just hadn't seemed like a good time to start questioning anyone—the pot calling the kettle black and all that. So he'd held his tongue and watched her pack. Later, Michael pleaded his case vehemently. Things had changed between them. They didn't talk anymore. He just needed someone to be with in a time of weakness. "She meant nothing to me...." But they all sounded like the same lame excuses any man would give when caught red-handed. The truth was the last thing he wanted to tell her. The truth was far too cold and too harsh. The truth was that they had done everything they had set out to do. They had managed to buy the perfect house and the expensive cars. They had become successful, the highly sought-after architect and the successful fashion designer wooed by every buyer in town. They had large bank accounts and stock options. They had cellular phones and Cartier watches. But something had been lost in the pursuit of all those things. They had lost each other. In bed at night they lay back to back like strangers. A quick peck somewhere near each other's lips and lights out. The lack of intimacy had started when Michael began insisting they have a child. They had talked about having children, but to Lauren, the time just wasn't right. Lauren knew this was what had started to diminish Michael's incurable romanticism and bring out the sarcastic asshole he had become.

Half of all marriages fall into ruin because of money. The other half because of sex. Michael and Lauren had money, but their sex life was taking a nose dive off a high cliff. Michael only wanted to make sweet and wonderful love to his beautiful wife in an effort to create a new life. Lauren, on the other hand, was starting to feel the need to explore more of her passion. She had a kinky side that he had never seen before. Her newly discovered boldness was starting to intimidate him. Michael could never imagine fucking his own wife, but Lauren's newfound sexuality had made him want to go out and find someone to fuck.

Michael tried to push the old memories back out of his head as he picked up the phone and dialed again. There was still no answer.

Lauren sat on Chance's lap in the small wooden director's chair inside the artist's booth. "I don't feel real comfortable with this," she said with an artificial smile on her face.

"No, please," the thin young man at the canvas begged. Just a little over five foot nine, he couldn't have weighed more than a hundred pounds soaking wet. He wore a red beret and a smock about three sizes too large for him, and was streaked with every conceivable color of the pastel chalk he had strewn around the booth. He was a messy artist, to say the least, but no doubt a talented one. "Just stay there a little bit longer. Perhaps even closer!"

"Like this?" Chance grabbed Lauren around her tiny waist and slid her wide hips closer to him. "Yeah, this'll work," he said with a light growl in his voice.

"That's it!" The kid went wild. Pieces of pastel chalk were flying everywhere as he worked furiously.

"Thanks for bringing me here," Chance whispered in Lauren's ear. His face was so close that she could feel his soft goatee tickling her cheek. "I had forgotten all about this."

That was a lie. He had been preparing his work for months and was looking forward to this year's art fair. In fact, he had already rented a booth in the same spot where he had displayed his photos for the past four years. Chance loved showing his work and hearing people rave about his artistic expression as seen through the lens of a camera.

"I still don't think we should be doing this," she said as she tried to pry herself out of Chance's grasp.

"No, please, stay still," the artist insisted. "Just a few more minutes."

"I'll pay you double if you make her sit here another twenty." Chance pulled Lauren even closer and allowed his hand to rest upon her thigh. The silky smoothness sent tingles throughout his body.

"Watchit," Lauren said through a clenched smile, trying to move Chance's hand away.

"Hold that!" the young artist exclaimed. "You two look terrific. The epitome of love and desire mixed with unbridled passion!" For a young man, this kid was pretty intuitive. Lauren felt the hot rush of crimson filling her cheeks and was grateful that her dark skin would hide her embarrassment.

"See, even he can see it." Chance's lips pressed against her earlobe as he spoke.

Lauren was completely flustered. She tried to rise, but Chance had a firm hold. "I really don't think I should be sitting here." Her mind searched for an excuse. "What about your leg? You must be in pain."

"Don't you worry about my leg." Chance had a mischievous look on his face. "My leg is very happy right now, as well as many other parts of my anatomy." His hand glided down the length of her thigh. "I could never forget how soft your skin was. I've missed that."

Lauren sprung up from her seat like a jack-in-the-box on the final note. sHer eyes shot a pained and icy glare in Chance's direction.

"Perfect!" the young artist crowed. His skinny arms shot up in the air in triumph. "And it's beautiful, if I do say so myself. Of course, it does help when you have such attractive models. You'd be surprised how many ugly people I have to draw every day."

Lauren stood by the side of the booth while Chance paid the artist for his work. She watched the small groups of people milling about the park's lush, green lawn, stopping at the booths and checking out the interesting wares of the up-and-coming artists. She wondered how many liaisons were taking place around them, how many other people here in the park were strolling hand in hand with some person other than their spouse? She thought about the creative stories and outright lies that were going to be told when some of these innocent-looking faces were confronted with, "how was your day today, honey? What did you do?"

Suddenly her eyes darted to every booth in the park, checking for anyone she might have known. Or even worse, anyone who knew her. She suddenly felt guilty, even though she knew she had done nothing wrong. All she had done was sit on a good friend's lap and allow an artist to draw their picture. Surely there was no harm in that. Of course, Michael would understand the innocence. But what about the quickening in her pulse as Chance leaned closer to her, whispering into her ear? How could she explain the tremble in her body as his soft lips brushed her cheek? And what about the power she felt growing inside him. A strength that pressed against the fabric of her short skirt and caused something inside her to melt into a warm flow upon white satin. He had missed the touch of her soft skin.

All of a sudden, Lauren felt herself gasping for breath. Even though she was outside, there didn't seem to be enough air in the world. There were too many people around, and a vexatious pounding was coming from the closet within her mind. The skeletons were trying to come out. Lauren took off running as fast as she could in no particular direction. She sped past the rows of white tent-like artists' booths that turned the park into a labyrinth of confusion. She rushed past groups of people who seemed to stare at her accusingly. She ran until she was out of the boundaries of the art fair and headed toward the lake. It would be quiet at the lake, she thought.It would be a perfect place to check all the locks in her mind, making sure no secret would escape.

"Lauren, wait up!" Chance yelled as he hobbled toward the lakeside. "You're making a man with a limp run after you. I don't think that's very considerate."

Breathless, Lauren stopped at the lake's edge and allowed Chance to catch up. "What are we doing here?" she asked. It was a rhetorical question but one that still needed an answer. "We promised each other we'd never go back there."

Lauren's eyes searched the still, blue water. The setting sun reflected off the surface a glimmering orange. It was peaceful here. Quiet. She wanted the silence to last forever.

"I'm sorry," Chance said, easing his way closer to her. "It's just that things are so different now. I understand things so much better. We knew it when we first met, you and I. We understood then that we should have been together. But something happened. Some strange twist of fate separated us and disrupted our destiny. You and I were meant to be together. And now that Roberta is gone..."

"Stop," her eyes pleaded with him. "Please don't do this. I am trying with every ounce of strength I have to pull my marriage back together. Please, let's not go back there. I married Michael and you married Roberta. That's just the way it is." Her words even sounded cold to her own ears. *The man's wife is dead, for Christ's sake.* "I miss her too." Her tone changed to deep compassion. "But you have to find your own way through this. And the answer is not in anything that may have happened between us."

"And I guess I'm just supposed to forget?" his eyes stared deep into her soul, searching for a hidden sign.

"It was a mistake." Her eyes stared back at him with conviction. It was the first truth she had allowed to come out of her mouth since their affair. "What happened between us was a mistake. I came to you that night when I had found out about Michael's affair, claiming that I wanted to talk to Roberta, but I knew she had a class. I knew she wasn't going to be home. I also knew what would happen if the two of us ever had enough time alone. And that's just what happened."

"So it was just a mistake." There was a slight shakiness in his voice. "An act of revenge." The thought was one he had feared all along. The two of them had shared a moment, a brief interlude of lust. But for Chance, the brief moment held a lifetime of dreams. He had always imagined holding Lauren, stroking every inch of her smooth soft skin. He had spent many nights thinking of her as he made love to Roberta. Those were the nights when he exploded in the most magnificent waves of blissful passion. But those nights were nothing in comparison to the night he actually made love to Lauren. It was everything he had ever dreamed of and more. She was wild and voracious and everything he had ever desired. And now she was telling him that it was all just a mistake.

"It wasn't just that," she knew her harsh words had sliced a piece out of him. What kind of persons was she to lash out at such a wonderful human being while he was in such pain? " I do love you."

Chance had already retreated into the room in his mind where he was safe. "So, we'll just make sure it doesn't happen again, huh?" He gave her a confident smile.

"Don't give me that," she said, seeing right through him. They both knew all too well the intense sexual energy between them. Chance was the man who had truly quenched her sexual desires. With him she had been able to let herself go and be as wild and wicked as she wanted. They were both insatiable, and the attraction had been growing stronger ever since he had moved back into their house. "What is it going to take?" she asked, as much to herself as to him. "Do you have to get hit by the train when it's headed your way before you get off the track?"

She took his hand and looked at him sternly. "I say we just nip it. Nip it, nip it, nip it!"

Chance couldn't help it. He tried as hard as he could to keep a straight face, but it was no use. Hysterical laughter exploded out of his tight lips.

"What's so funny?" she asked, still holding that stern look and furrowed brow.

"Nip it?" Chance was still fighting through his laughter.

"I'm serious."

"Yeah, but you gotta admit, 'nip it' does sound a little funny." Chance struggled to get his laughter under control.

"My mother used to say 'nip it' and there was nothing funny about it." Lauren was dead serious. Her mother Lorraine was a devout Christian woman with a deep Catholic upbringing, who never let a foul word cross her lips. When she was really peeved, like when her husband Lenny Rose would come tipping home in the wee hours of the morning smelling of cheap alcohol and spirited women, or when her son Phil, Lauren's only sibling, would get caught skipping school and smoking that "reefer," Lorraine would spew ou,t "Nip it!" in such a way that it took on the same meaning as, "All right now everybody cut the shit!"

A bright, honest smile lingered on Chance's face. It was a strong, handsome face with chiseled features. The slight hint of a goatee, his artistic pride and joy, traced around his soft, full lips and framed his strong, rectangular chin. Light twinkled in his dark brown eyes. Lauren couldn't help smiling back.

"You are so bad," she said, falling toward him and ending up in his arms. She started to back away quickly, but he gave her a comforting look that said it was all right. She was in a safe place and nothing bad could ever happen there. He wrapped his arm around her, and they continued walking along the shore of the lake.

"I've lost everything I ever loved." Chance's voice sounded lost and disconnected. "Today, some man I don't even know tried to put a price tag on the lives of my wife and child. I don't know where I'm going or what I'm doing half the time, and I'm just breathing out of habit. The only thing I have left is friendship. I need you to be my friend, to hold my hand and watch the sunset and give me strength to make it another day."

What was she supposed to say to that? What else could she do but hold this man's hand? They stopped and shared a lingering gaze. The sun was setting behind them, their bodies etched in silhouette. A loon glided over the crystal lake.

"I don't think that this is how two friends watch the sunset," she said, as she felt their bodies drawing closer together.

"Well, we're close friends." Chance's answer was short in hopes of not disturbing the moment.

There was hardly any space between them. "Very close, I'd say," she said, starting to fidget.

"And most people aren't as fortunate to have friends as beautiful and enchanting as you." He was pouring it on thick.

"And it's kind of chilly." She was turning into the fly playing too close to the web. "We're just keeping each other warm."

"Very warm...hot...wet." His lips barely touched hers, like the wings of a butterfly's kiss.

Suddenly, Lauren snapped her head to the side, burying her cheek in Chance's chest. "I think I hear a train coming," she mumbled breathlessly, as she closed her eyes and searched for strength.

"How could you just turn away from me like that?" Chance's lips still longed for hers.

"Let me tell you something," she released a heavy sigh. "It ain't easy."

Nine

The living room was dark, except for the soft moonbeams through the large picture window. Michael sat alone in the darkness, staring beyond the grand entry, his eyes fixed on the front door. It was quarter to ten. Not that late by any adult standards, but much too late for him not to know his wife's whereabouts. He had already checked his voice mail, both at work and at home, and there was no word from either Lauren or Chance. He had also double-checked the battery in his pager and had even paged himself to make sure it was working. There was just no excuse for Lauren not to have contacted him.

His hand trembled slightly as he poured himself another glass of liquid relaxation from the oval decanter. A few drops spilled on the small antique end table. He wiped up the spilled liquid with the tips of his fingers and then sucked it off his fingertips, one by one. He made a loud smacking sound as he pulled his index finger from between his tight lips, pursed in an angry scowl. At two hundred and eighty bucks a bottle, he wasn't about to waste a single drop. He had been saving the expensive bottle of

Courvoisier for a special occasion. He remembered seeing it in the locked glass case when he and Lauren strolled through the local JHP Wine and Spirits. They were looking for a special bottle of wine to take over to Chance and Roberta's the night they got the news about the pregnancy. Michael thought the bottle of Courvoisier would go great with a couple of Cohibas he had stashed away. He had planned to break them out the day Roberta had the baby, so that he and Chance could celebrate in style. That special moment was now lost forever, and he could think of no reason not to open that expensive bottle now.

The light-golden liquid passed soothingly over his lips, but burst into flames inside his mouth and burned like hell as it slid down his throat. He thought about going to get a couple of ice cubes from the fridge, but he didn't want to move away from his prime seat. He wanted to be there when she and Chance walked into the house. He wanted to greet them with a smile and say, "Welcome home, glad to see the two of you are all right. It's good to have you back, safe and sound. Did you eat yet? I haven't and I'm starving." He wanted to say those things, but in the back of his mind, he knew he wouldn't.

He sat the short, stocky highball glass back on the table. His hand still trembled for some reason. He wasn't nervous. He was sure he was in complete control. He was obviously paying no attention to that thing inside his chest that was pounding against his shirt. Nor did it faze him that the blood inside his veins was pumping so hard you could see the thin, pulsating lines bulging from his temples.

The keys made a rattling sound in the lock of the front door. Michael's head jerked up and leaned to the side like a watchdog listening for an intruder. He watched the latch of the deadbolt turn more slowly than he had ever seen anything move in his life. He fought back the urge to charge the front door and snatch it open, grabbing whatever was on the other side and slamming it into one of the foyer walls.

The door glided open silently, allowing the two closely huddled shadows to step into the darkness. There was giggling amid the shuffling of feet and the clicking of high heels on the marble floor. Michael could tell from the sound of the heels that Lauren was wearing those damn CFMP's he hated so much. Not only did they make her legs look longer and more attractive to every cockhound walking the streets, they also made her an inch and a half taller than him.

Lauren flipped the switch near the front door, filling the room with harsh white light. She and Chance both froze at the sight of the angry man sitting alone in the dark.

"So, somebody want to tell me what the hell is going on?" All the planned pleasantries had fled Michael's mind.

"Michael, what are you doing sitting here in the dark?" Her voice shook slightly.

"It just seemed appropriate, Lauren, honey. I'm in the dark about so many things. But now I think I'm beginning to see the light." Michael's hand trembled noticeably as he reached for his glass. "You'all want to shed a little more light and tell me where the hell you've been all day?"

Lauren felt an argument coming on. Her mind quickly shot into battle mode. But when she looked into Michael's eyes, she didn't see the anger and fury she expected. Instead, she saw hurt and betrayal. All of a sudden her mind went blank.

"You remember, don't you?" She felt herself stuttering. "Chance had to meet with the attorney today. They wanted to make him an offer. It's a pretty good offer too, according to the attorney, and I think Chance might accept it...isn't that right?" She was babbling and she knew it. She looked to Chance for help but he was too involved in a staring match with Michael.

"Well hip-hip-hoo-fucking-rah for Chance." The anger in Michael's voice started to surface now. "That attorney of yours keeps pretty late hours, doesn't he?" He stared Chance down like a heavyweight fighter sizing up his opponent.

The air in the room was so thick you could scoop it up with a spoon. "It was just a nice day," Lauren added. "We went out to celebrate."

"To celebrate, huh?" Michael turned his glare toward her. "And in what phoneless principality did you go to celebrate? Obviously there were no phones around because you didn't even try to call me."

"It's my fault, man, I'm sorry." Chance thought if he took the blame, perhaps things would go better for Lauren. "We went by the art fair." It sounded innocent enough. "My leg was feeling pretty good, and I just wanted to take a walk."

"Oh, so your leg's all better now, huh?" Michael stepped up to Chance. The two of them hadn't shared many words since their incident, and, suddenly, Michael felt the need to flex his muscles. "Well, then, since you can finally stand on your own two feet, perhaps you can stop using my wife as a goddamn crutch!"

"Michael!" Lauren said, stepping between them.

"No, don't." Chance put a reassuring hand on Lauren's shoulder. "Let him say what he has to say. He needs to get it out."

Chance's calm and monotone voice only angered Michael more. "And you need to walk your ass back up to that all-night attorney's office, get your check and get the fuck out of my house."

Michael was inches from Chance's face. Chance could smell the pungent odor on Michael's breath. He was amazed how much it smelled like rubbing alcohol. The acrid odor reminded him of his childhood. His home had always smelled like a distillery and his mother, no matter what time of day, always reeked. A picture of her flashed into his mind, her dark, blotchy skin and red swollen eyes, the ever-present Kool Filter King 100 jutting from her gray, chapped lips, that old gray housecoat with the four missing buttons and the grease stain in the front. He wondered if she'd ever washed that housecoat. Chance shook off the memory and turned his eyes back to Michael. "Is that it?"

"Yeah, that about sizes it up." Michael pushed his way past Chance and headed up the stairs.

Lauren looked cataleptic. Her brain had shut down, but her eyes continued to shift back and forth between Chance and the direction in which Michael had stormed off.

"He's right, you know," Chance said calmly. "It is time for me to go."

"Not like this." The numbness in her head started to drift. "We've all been through too much to end it all like this."

She blinked rapidly, her mind trying to take in all that had just happened. *What right did Michael have to go off like that?* she thought. *Nothing happened. The whole afternoon was completely innocent. What exactly was he trying to say?* Lauren pushed her way pass Chance and headed up after Michael.

The door to the master bedroom slammed shut with such a boom that one of the pictures in the hallway fell and crashed to the floor. Lauren stepped over the broken glass, charged into the bedroom and gave the door a slam of her own.

"What the hell is your problem?" she demanded. She was still holding the rolled-up poster-board in her hand. She threw the drawing down on the bed. She wanted to have her hands free for this heated debate.

Michael looked curiously at the paper cylinder with the bright-orange rubber band. He reached for it. Ice water suddenly pumped through Lauren's veins. She tried to snatch the drawing back, but Michael kept it out of reach. She gave up the struggle quickly, and the two of them stared at one another for an eternity as Michael slowly moved the rubber band up the length of the paper.

Lauren swallowed hard as Michael unrolled the poster-sized paper and stared at the drawing of his wife and what had been his best friend. The picture was the kind young lovers had done to commemorate their first date—two people with faces pressed close together, smiles and happiness. The kind of picture newlyweds hang proudly on the wall of their first apartment and then, months later, rush to toss in the trash during the heat of an ugly breakup. Michael searched his mind to recall whether he and Lauren had ever posed for one of these pictures together.

"What the fuck is this all about?" he snapped, obviously hurt.

"You want to try and keep your voice down?" Lauren asked, trying to change focus.

"Do you want to try and explain this shit to me?"

"You don't have to yell."

"I just want you to tell me what the hell is going on here, Lauren."

"Nothing—there's nothing going on." She had a flutter in her voice, the kind that usually comes into play when people are trying desperately to hide something. "And I would appreciate it if you wouldn't talk to me like I was some kind of dog."

Michael walked closer to her and had to tip his head back slightly to look up into her eyes. *Goddammit*, he thought, *she does have on those damn high heels.* "Well, if you're going to run around like some bitch in heat, you should expect to be spoken to like one."

Lauren tried to hit the playback button in her mind. Had he just called her a bitch? It was the first time Michael had ever cursed her. Oh, she knew at times he could have a pretty foul mouth, she could too for that matter, but as far as she could recollect, this was the first time he had called her out of her name. *A bitch...me?* she thought. She began to feel her mother rise up inside her, and she had an urge to take Michael into the bathroom and wash his mouth out with a bar of soap.

"Can we be civil here?" She had that calming tone in her voice. "Chance is right downstairs."

"I don't give a fuck where Chance is. I want the muthafucka to get the fuck out of my house!" Michael made sure the last part of his statement was aimed directly at the closed door and loud enough for Chance to hear.

"You're the one who asked him to stay here. You were the martyr." She was standing up for Chance again, but this time she didn't care. "You were the one who was going to repay your sins by taking in your best friend and seeing him through his time of misery."

"It was the least I could do."

"So now what? You've done your least, so now get the fuck out of your house?"

"Hey, beating the shit out of me and screwing my wife wasn't part of the deal."

Michael's words sent an icy chill through the room. Lauren couldn't believe what she had just heard.

"That's a pretty large accusation, Michael," she said, trying to remain calm. "Because if you're accusing Chance, then you're accusing me, too."

Michael didn't want to continue the conversation. He wasn't trying to accuse her of anything. There wasn't one fiber in his soul that wanted to believe his sweet and beautiful wife would have betrayed him. But there was still an uneasy feeling in the pit of his stomach.

"Is that what you're doing?" Lauren couldn't let it go. "Are you accusing me of having an affair with Chance?"

A memory suddenly surfaced from the depths of Michael's mind. It was a memory of troubled Roberta confiding in him in search of answers. He and Roberta had been close, but never close enough for her to ask him the sort of thing she was asking. He remembered thinking that Roberta had been completely out of line and acting a little paranoid. He had reassured her that everything was fine between her and Chance. He reassured her because he was sure it was. That was before now. "You know, Roberta suspected that Chance was having an affair," Michael started. "But I told her, 'no way', not Chance. I'm his best friend. I would have known...He would have told me." Michael's voice started to trail off into some dark ally of a memory as he reconstructed the past in his mind. "Unless..." It was all starting to make sense now. "Was it you?"

Lauren got an immediate defensive look on her face. "What the hell are you talking about?"

"You heard me." He knew that repeating a question he had just asked or giving him that innocent "What are you talking about?" crap was usually her way of trying to get out of something. "Was it you?" he repeated. "Did you fuck my best friend?"

KA-PAP! The palm of Lauren's hand landed on the side of Michael's face even before she realized she was taking a swing. Her palm turned bright red and stung as if she had just grabbed hold of a live wire. Michael's head rolled back slowly to look at her. His eyes cut through her like ginsu knives as he fought back the raging desire to allow his slowly clenching fist to fly and send her sailing across the room.

"I hope that's a 'No,'" Michael said, completely disregarding her attack.

Michael turned and headed out the bedroom door. He was leaving, and that was that. He was turning his back to her and walking out of the door. For a brief second she considered telling

him everything. He was right. Roberta's suspicions were right.
She and Chance did have an affair. She wanted to tell him the
whole truth. How the first time was just after she had found out
about Michael's affair. How it all started out as a way to get back
at him. She wanted to tell him how it turned into something over-
powering and uncontrollable. She wanted to tell him that she and
Chance had been together quite a few times during the time she
and Michael were separated and that Chance had allowed her to
explore her wild and dark side. She wanted to tell him that it was
over, and she had gotten it out of her system. She was ready to be
good now. A good wife. A perfect wife. But how could she tell
him the whole truth? She was sure that he would want the truth,
the whole truth and nothing but the truth. And there was no way
she could ever let him know the whole truth.

Chance left the house shortly after the argument reached
screaming proportions. He didn't see how he could be of any use
there and knew his presence would only make things worse.
Besides, Michael had told him to get out. He figured he would go
back in the morning and pick up his things, but right now he felt
better walking alone down the dark sidewalkless street.

He glanced down the driveway of each house he passed. The
huge, sprawling homes had enormous front yards, each one more
perfectly landscaped than the last. Each driveway boasted
expensive cars in a flashy display of success. *Boujie assholes,* he
thought as he continued walking towards the main road. An old
Beatles' tune popped into his head, and, immediately, he heard
himself whistling the melody of "Money Can't Buy Me Love." He
reached the main highway and caught a ride with an elderly
gentleman in a dusty, old powder-blue Chevy.

The elderly man talked non-stop for over an hour and didn't
once push the old whining engine over forty—even while driving

in the fast lane of the expressway. Several times, Chance fought
back the urge to slam his own foot on top of the driver's dusty old
boot, flooring the accelerator to keep up with the passing traffic.
But this creeping pace wasn't all bad. It gave Chance time to think.
Time to plan just what he needed to do next.

"So, where ya headed?" the elderly man asked in a scratchy
voice.

It was a good question. A logical question, but, unfortunately,
one Chance hadn't given too much thought to. He rubbed his face
with the palm of his hand, inhaling and exhaling deeply. He could
still smell Lauren's scent on his skin. It was sweet and soothing
like the night air after a summer rain.

"Fifth and Main," Chance said finally and then smiled
peacefully. *That's where I should have been staying all along,* he
thought to himself. It had always been his special little home away
from home.

Ten

The second story of the abandoned warehouse that sat on the unlit corner of Fifth and Main had been the place Chance had called his sanctuary for the past four years. He had fixed up the old dilapidated warehouse with an art deco paint job, an old coffee table and sofa, a stove and dinette set, and the old canopied four-poster that he and Roberta had brought for their first apartment and then traded for an elaborate bedroom suite. His favorite multi colored, fabric-worn wing back chair sat alone in the center of the room.

A series of windows lined the four walls, giving way to a panoramic view of a forgotten and decaying section of the city. The area was seedy, impoverished by grit and grime. Most people sped by it while doing sixty-five on the nearby I-95. They never gave it a glance. Yet it was the place where Chance found the most comfort and did his best work. Perhaps it was the fact that it was forgotten and neglected that gave him his deep felt inspiration. It reminded him of his childhood and all the disjointed images from a fragmented past. Those were the things he photographed the best. Those were the things he saw through his camera lens that no one else could comprehend.

Chance had started his career as a staff photographer for a local magazine. He had soon grown tired of the still photos of perfect families congregating in the park, the politicians making speeches in the square, the unimaginative recounting of Labor Day parades and the grand openings of shopping centers. He had started to see something different through the lens of his camera. A twisted view of life that the editors of the magazine just couldn't grasp. He started to distort images to recreate the "true meaning" of the things he saw. He added his own interpretation of art to every frame of his celluloid canvas. Though these photographs gained him accolades from the artistic community, they were a bit too avant-garde for the magazine's taste, and he was soon asked to leave.

Leaving the magazine proved to be the best thing that could have happened to him. In no time at all, Chance became the talk of every local art show in town and was highly touted for his bold and unusual style. He turned out work so furiously that the small home he shared with Roberta was no longer able to house his art and their lives at the same time. It was Roberta who suggested he find himself a studio.

Now, here he stood in the center of the room surrounded by walls of cold concrete and beams of imperturbable steel. This was once the place that had always offered him peace in times of turmoil. The special place where he could always get in touch with his emotions. But today, unlike any other time in his life, as he stood in the center of this room, he just felt alone.

Wild music came crashing out of the bookshelf speakers placed in each corner of the room. The sounds were fantastic and disjointed, as if Miles Davis and Amadeus Mozart were battling for attention in front of a raving audience while standing on the same stage. Chance stood in front of his latest piece of creative genius, a mastery of art and technology in a display of digital photographic images over a huge collection of monitors.

The monitors took up most of a wall and were arranged in various shapes and sizes from floor to ceiling. Unconnected pictures grew from the center monitor and then started to strobe out at random over the others to create one huge, spectacular image. Then, just before the eye could grasp hold of it, the monitors would burst off into several entities of their own in an explosion of light. Chance stared at the glowing monitors as his long, black silk robe cocooning his body fell gracefully to the floor.

He stood naked in front of the monitors, his face filled with a new sense of purpose. The images on the monitors continued to flash, an arm, an eye, a polished fingernail. What looked like the structural framework of a woman's form twirled in a monitor in the top corner. A blastocyst of color exploded from the row of monitors on the floor and sent sparkling pixels into their counterparts. The image grew and started to take shape. Graceful lines and contours etched out the soft features of a beautiful face with large brown eyes, succulent lips and dimples that accented either side of a sensual smile. The image was a huge photograph of Lauren's face. She stared back at him, drawing him like a moth to a flame.

Chance slowly approached the wall of monitors as they exploded into several individual pictures of Lauren. He stretched his arms out and pressed his naked flesh against the cold glowing, screens. Beads of perspiration seeped from his pores and dripped down his muscular back, making his body glisten in the light. A rush of tingling sensations rippled over his skin as he pressed harder against the glass in a mad attempt to melt into it. He closed his eyes and thought about her. Beckoned her. Prayed to her.

Chance didn't know how long he had been standing at the wall of monitors when he heard the incessant pounding on the front door that matched the throbbing in his temples. The sound jarred him back to a hazy sense of reality. He slipped back into his robe and slowly headed down the long corridor and down a narrow stairwell to the front door.

His face was placid, void of any emotions, when he opened the door and found Lauren standing there.

"I knew you'd be here," she said with an edge of desperation in her voice.

"I knew you'd come." His voice was disturbingly calm.

"We have to talk." Lauren's eyes quickly searched the streets, checking to see if any prying eyes were watching. She saw nothing. Not a soul, not a car, not even a wandering stray. She slipped through the door and stepped into the cold, dark stairwell. Chance pushed the door closed slowly and the latch whispered shut.

"Michael knows something." Her remorse filled the air. "I'm not sure how much he knows, but he knows something happened between us."

Chance stared back at her. His empty look went unchanged. Lauren wasn't sure if he had heard what she had just said.

"He said Roberta knew also." Tears started to fill in her eyes. Chance moved closer to her in the dark, narrow space. He looked deeply into her sorrowful eyes.

"And what about the baby?" he asked. "Do you think either of them knew about the baby?"

The tears started to fall like forbidden lovers leaping from jagged cliffs. "Oh my God, what have we done?" Her head was suddenly too heavy. The sad rush of memories filled her mind all at once, forcing her head to fall into her hands. "Michael can never find out about that. Our marriage is barely holding together as it is, and if he ever found out about that baby..." Her voice trailed off into a barren wasteland of silence.

It had happened just three months after she and Michael had separated. Her period had been only a few days late, but before this, she could have launched rockets with her monthly sense of precision. She had driven clear across town that day in hopes of finding a pharmacy where no one would recognize her.

She had felt like a wanted criminal as she stood in the checkout line adjusting her baseball cap down low over her eyebrows and pushing up the black-tinted shades to cover her eyes. She had placed a few other items on the conveyor in hopes of hiding what she had really come for. On the conveyor sat several miscellaneous items, but the small pastel pink box stood out like a red flag and seemed to say, "Hey look at this, it's an EARLY PREGNANCY TEST KIT!" Lauren tried to think positively as she pushed the package of Maxi-pads in front of the EPT box. *What an insane contradiction in products,* she thought. *It's like those people who stand in line at the grocery store buying low-cal frozen entrées to go along with the Sara Lee double-decker chocolate cake.*

There were three test kits in the box, and as Lauren sat in the restroom stall of the Arco station, she allowed the final test strip from the box to fall weightlessly to the floor. The tip of the strip was a bright blue, and she finally accepted the undeniable truth. She was, without a doubt, pregnant. A wave of nausea hit her suddenly, but she was sure that it wasn't the queasiness associated with morning sickness. This sudden urge to puke her guts out was the product of sheer panic. She couldn't remember the last time she and Michael had made love, but she did realize that there was a good chance that this was not his child. The contents of her stomach erupted in a painful explosion of despair.

She and Michael had been talking about getting back together. He had apologized endlessly and sworn his love to her. He had promised her that things would be better if she would just give it one more try. He desperately wanted their marriage to work. How would she explain this pregnancy to him? How could she ever expect him to understand and take her back with open arms? There was only one thing she could do.

As she sat alone in the sterile waiting room of the woman's clinic, she thought back on the twelve years of all-girl parochial school that her parents forced upon her. "Young girls can get themselves into trouble hanging around those demonic boys," she could hear her mother's straight-laced voice warn. "They're only after one thing, and when they get you in trouble, they're nowhere to be found." Lauren checked the empty seat next to her. Her mother was right. Here she was in trouble and all alone. She suddenly felt like that little girl dressed in the red tam and plaid skirt all over again. She could envision the statues of St. Timothy and St. Christopher staring down at her. How many sins had she committed over the past few weeks? How many Hail Marys and Our Fathers did she need to say to get out of this one?

It was a cold and rainy late afternoon when she stepped out of the Just For Her clinic. The overcast sky made everything dark and dreary as if God had stripped the world of color and painted every-thing a dark lifeless gray. The pit of her stomach ached from the emptiness inside of her. But that pain was nothing compared to the agony she felt in her heart. Someone had just sucked life out of her, ripped it from within her womb and deposited it into a nearby receptacle. The rain hit her face and mixed with the tears as she looked toward the sky. She wanted to scream. She wanted to die. It was the worst day in her life.

The tears were now flowing down her face in endless streams as she glanced back up at Chance. The darkness of the dank stairwell made it difficult to see his face. "Swear to me that this stays between us," she pleaded with him. "Promise me that Michael never finds out."

"He won't," Chance promised. He took her into his arms and held her tight. She returned his embrace with one of her own.

"It's over, Chance," she said. "No more lies, no more secrets. It's over. I came to say good-bye."

Chance clung to her tighter. His face nuzzled against her soft cheek, soaking away her tears with his skin. "It's okay," he whispered. "He won't find out, I promise. Just please don't leave me. Just please don't say good bye." His words were desperate. "I need you. Don't let him do this to us. I need you in my life."

"Chance, I'm sorry."

"No," Chance demanded. "I'll take care of Michael, just...please."

Lauren tried to pull away. Tried to pry herself from Chance's embrace. "Chance, no," she insisted. "This has to end now."

But Chance wasn't letting go, not in his mind and definitely not with his arms. He snatched her hard, making her body slam into his. His lips pressed against the side of her face. Hard wet kisses that started to trail down her neck.

"No," she pleaded. "Stop-please."

His hard, passionate kisses continued. He forced her back against the wall. His hands started roaming her body. Her small hands and frail arms tried to push him away but only managed to rip the sheer silk robe away from his shoulders. His muscular shoulders leaned into her. His bare skin pressed against her face. She could taste the salty sweetness of his glistening skin as she tried to battle the burning desire growing within her.

"Chance, please..."

His lips engulfed hers, swallowing her words and muffling her cries. His tongue danced around hers, tantalizing her senses. Lauren tried to turn away, but now she was not only fighting Chance, she was also fighting herself.

"No...no" she repeated the words over and over again. But she didn't actually hear the words come out of her mouth and wondered if she had said them out loud at all.

Chance slammed her back against the wall. She could feel the cold sensation of the musty wall on her back as her blouse was peeled away from her skin. She felt Chance's lips kissing her breast. She prayed that she was still saying "no," but the only thing she could hear was heavy breathing and moans of pleasure. Moans that were coming from her own lips. Damn her body for betraying her own mind. *What the hell am I doing and why can't I stop?*

She cursed the demons inside her, pleaded with them to go away. But Chance had replaced the demons and was now inside of her, plunging deep and hard. Her hips moved in unison with his, matching each powerful thrust. Her arms strained to cling to him tightly. Her mind was gone now, completely void of thought...unbridled lust had taken its place.

Eleven

L auren shot upright in the bed, her eyes darting around the room. The familiarity that greeted her eyes had a calming effect. The soft-white walls were accented by paintings in whitewashed frames, flowing chiffon curtains covered the windows and filtered in the warmth of the sun, crisp white sheets with pink and lavender flowers surrounded her. She was home, safe and sound in her own bed.

She remembered being grateful that Michael had not been home to see her arrive at such an ungodly hour. She had removed her clothes quickly and climbed into bed. She had wanted to take a shower, but thought it would look strange if Michael were to come home. How on earth could she explain taking a shower at two in the morning?

Yet here it was early morning, and still Michael's side of the bed was untouched. *He has some nerve,* she thought, *staying out all night.* But the thought was quickly erased by thoughts of her own guilt.

She rolled over and sat up on the edge of the bed. Her

97

reflection stared back at her from the oval mirror across the room. It was hard to believe that the haggard, worried, guilt-ridden woman in the mirror was her own reflection. Looking at herself made her feel dirty-soiled, unworthy of the chaste white that surrounded her. She tried to stand, but her legs felt wobbly and her body felt surprisingly heavy, as if she had gained a hundred pounds during the night. She wondered if guilt could actually weigh a person down. If sins came with an actual mass that the sinner would be burdened to carry for the rest of his or her life. For the first time in her life, she wished she could have been more like her mother.

Lauren's mother was the purest among pure, a God-fearing woman who seldom went a day without picking up a Bible and finding some scripture to give her strength. Lorraine had been brought up in a Christian home and believed that everything she did was in the name of the Father. She practically lived at church, and to her being late to early mass was a major sin. The woman was a saint and Lord only knows how she ended up with the likes of Lenny Rose.

Lauren's father was a drop-dead gorgeous man, more on the pretty side than the rugged. He had wavy hair and the deepest dimples anyone had ever seen on a man, a trait he passed on to Lauren. He exuded sexuality from every pore—another trait Lauren had woefully received—and was quite a ladies' man. His escapades had become legendary in the neighborhood where they lived. His tipping out late at night and then staggering in early in the morning became a routine. He was known to have slept with most of the attractive women who were always hanging around him, and he lived for his weekend trips to Vegas, where some people said he had another family on the side.

Lorraine was a forgiving woman. She threw no stones and would accuse no one of sins. She kept her place as a wife, being subservient to her husband, and never thought a vengeful thought, never considered for one moment giving her cheating husband a taste of his own medicine.

Why couldn't I have been more like my mom? Lauren thought as she stood slowly and headed toward the shower.

Michael felt a shooting pain begin somewhere in his lower back that sent agonizing twinges to the base of his neck. This was the first time he had slept on a sofa in years, and the art deco design in his office wasn't actually built for comfort. He tried to stretch out his body, but the sharp, stabbing pain quickly brought his arms back to his side. It had been a long night, a night of tossing and turning, and retracing the steps of his and Lauren's relationship, trying to remember just where they had stumbled. He guessed it wasn't just one thing that caused them to drift apart, but a long series of events. It was all the arguments they had never concluded and had conveniently swept under the proverbial rug. It was all the differences of opinion that they had chosen to ignore and pretend that everything was just fine. They had bought into the lie that they were the perfect couple, the couple who had it all. The luckiest couple on earth. But it all had become a façade. A phony veil that had become cumbersome and uncomfortable to wear like a wool sweater on a hot summer day.

The honest-to-God truth was that they were not perfect. Far from it. They had the same problems everyone else did. But the absence of problems isn't what makes a marriage work, it's the tenacity of the couple who face the problems head on that survive this lifelong commitment called marriage. They had been running away from their problems for too long. They had both made mistakes and had expended too much energy trying to pretend those mistakes had never happened. What had become of "love, honor, and cherish?" What had happened to that tingling sensation he used to get when he touched her hand and laced his fingers through hers? When did he stop sending her flowers, and when did she stop kissing him goodnight and then pulling his arm around her like a warm, cozy blanket?

"You do have to be friends," he said out loud. It was a revelation as if he had just discovered plutonium. Two friends who are deeply in love, that is what marriage is all about, he realized. sometimes friends don't see eye-to-eye, and sometimes they go their separate ways, but true friends are forever, and he and Lauren were forever..

Michael's head spun with excitement. He knew he didn't have all the answers, and he realized he was becoming a bit melodramatic. He had never been the type of person who would sit up and ponder the meaning of life and the depths of his character, but the insight he had just gained was powerful. For once he had searched his own soul and discovered what he truly wanted, not what was best for everyone else. This was what was best for him.

The front door to his office swung open in a quick fluid swish as Janice entered the room. She froze when she saw Michael. "Mr. Hubbs," she said. "What'd you do, sleep here?"

Michael noticed the clean coffee mug, the morning paper and the stack of files in her arms, the same items that greeted him every morning when he came to work. He had never before stopped to think about how those items appeared on his desk with daily precision. It was as if some "office fairy" floated in during the wee hours of the morning, placed the items neatly on his desk and then floated away on silken angelic wings. He never realized it before, but he was now looking into the soft eyes of that angelic fairy, and her name was Janice. "You know, I'd be lost without you." Michael said to her as he smiled an appreciative smile. "I'll get to that stuff later," he continued, with a huge grin on his face. "Right now I've got some things to take care of at home."

Michael headed toward the door, stopped on his way out and gave Janice a big juicy kiss on the lips. Janice blinked her eyes blankly about twenty times before her mind kicked back in. She watched Michael's long strides as he headed out of the office. There was a spring in his step, the kind of rhythmic stride that black men often get when they are feeling really good about themselves. Michael stopped at the vase of fresh-cut flowers on Janice's desk. Daffodils and marigolds were surrounded by baby's breath. *Perfect,* Michael thought, and scooped the flowers up in his hands.

"Janice," he said walking toward the elevators. "Would you please call my house and let my wife know that I'm on my way home?"

The steam wafting out of the shower filled the bathroom, covering the glass with a fine cloudy mist. Lauren stood inside the massive shower stall that was comfortably large enough for two. The dual showerheads poured out, pulsating streams of warm liquid relaxation. Lauren threw back her head, closed her eyes and relished the warm spray. The pounding water shielded her from the world beyond the steamy glass walls. She tried to wash away her thoughts, to close her eyes and scrub away the stench of sin from her flesh. She gave herself completely to the falling water, hoping that its torrent would make her pure once more. She was so entrenched in her own world that she didn't hear the metallic shrill of the phone ringing in the next room. Nor did she hear the soft click downstairs as the front door closed shut.

Light footsteps gently tapped on the marble floor of the foyer and then made their way up the stairs. Without a sound, they crept across the plush softness of the bedroom carpet and made their way toward the master bathroom. The strong muscular hand pushed the bathroom door open slightly, giving way to the sight of

Lauren's wet and naked body beyond the glass walls. She was beautiful. The soft curves of her supple body appeared in silhouette upon the steamy glass. Her hand glided sensuously over her soft, wet skin. Her white satin panties were lying on the floor in the doorway. The long fingers of the man's hand picked up the satin treasure and brought them to his face. He inhaled the nectar deeply, allowing the panties to linger on his open lips. With his other hand, he reached into his pants and slowly began to stroke himself, each gentle stroke sending pulsating pleasure throughout his body. A low, guttural moan escaped his throat.

Lauren sensed the presence of someone standing outside the shower. "Michael?" she called. But there was no answer. She tried to peer out of the glass but the fog was too thick.

"Uhmmm." She heard it again, and this time she was sure someone was in the room. She quickly cleared a circle in the glass and peered through. Her eyes tried to pierce the thick fog, but the steam filled the circle in the window just as quickly as she could clear it. Finally her eyes caught sight of something that made her blood run cold.

Chance was standing in the doorway staring at her, his hand shoved down the front of his pants and a glistening pool of drool forming in the corner of his mouth. Lauren wanted to scream, but her mind couldn't remember how. She shoved the shower door open and grabbed a towel that was lying near the bathroom basin. Was he insane? she thought, what the fuck was he thinking? What if Michael had come home and seen him standing there like that? She wrapped her dripping body with the towel and then turned toward the door to read Chance the riot act, but he was gone. The doorway was empty and there was no sign of him anywhere in the room.

Lauren stormed through the bedroom, her dripping body leaving a trail of tiny wet footprints behind her. She charged past the door into the upstairs hallway and ran right into - Michael.

"Michael?" She didn't mean for it to come out so much like a question. "What are you doing here?" She tried to clean it up. What she really wanted to say was, "How long have you been here, and did you see what the fuck your sick ass friend was doing while I was in the shower?"

"We've got some things to talk about," Michael said.

This didn't sound good to her. There were too many things that they could have to talk about, and right now, none that she could think of were any good. She looked at him curiously as he handed her a bouquet of flowers.

"I did a lot of thinking last night," he started right in. "Tried to answer a lot of questions that I had in my mind: questions about us, questions about things that happened. But I guess the main question was whether or not I wanted to be in this relationship anymore."

Lauren tried to give Michael her undivided attention but couldn't stop her eyes from searching the house or her mind from wondering where the hell Chance was.

Michael took a gentle hold of her shoulders and looked deep into her eyes. "You mean more to me than anyone or anything I've ever known. You are my best friend and I love you. I've decided that this relationship, our marriage, is the single most important thing in my life." He had her undivided attention now. "I made a decision to fight for this marriage and to try and work things out between us. But I can't do it on my own. I came home to find out what you want to do. I need to know if you want to fight for this relationship, or walk away."

It was the first time that Michael had talked to her like this in years. It was the first time in awhile that he had truly said what was on his mind. The words felt good to her. Their meaning had touched something inside her she had thought was long gone. She looked into his eyes and they said truly, "I love you." She tried to speak but the words got caught in the flood of joyous tears that began to run down her face. She continued her futile attempt to speak and finally expressed her feeling inside the comfort of a tight, unending embrace. She could feel the warmth of his love coming from his body, and right now, she needed him so much. Michael started to pull away, but she continued to cling to him, never wanting this moment to end.

Michael and Lauren sat and talked for hours. It was the closest the two of them had been in years. Michael shared with her his most intimate secrets and darkest fears. She watched him closely as he spoke, gazing deep into his warm eyes. Listening carefully to his every word, she was swept away by the soothing calm of his voice. She admired his honesty, reveled in the strength and conviction of his words. She wondered if she too could ever be that honest. She doubted it.

Occasionally Lauren's eyes wandered around the room, checking for shadows in distant corners. But there was no sign of Chance. Perhaps he had left. Maybe he had slipped out the back door while she and Michael were lost in deep conversation. She hoped that Chance had hung around long enough to overhear some of the things that she and Michael had said. She prayed that he had heard her as she and Michael said how much they truly loved each other. How much they wanted their marriage to work. They spoke about forgiveness and their commitment to one another. They talked openly about the newfound devotion they swore would never end. They held hands and shared warm and loving smiles. She wished silently that Chance had been there to see that. Maybe then he would understand and allow her to return to what she knew in her heart was the right place.

Michael regretted having to go back to work. The two of them stood in the grand foyer at the front door gazing at one another.

"You know, I really don't want to go back to work," Michael said, his eyes scanning every inch of her beautiful face. "I just can't get out of this meeting."

"You go on and take care of business." Lauren's voice was reassuring. "I'll have dinner ready for you when you get home."

"I think I could go for eating a little something when I get back." He had a sly look on his face. "But it ain't nothing you're gonna want to put on a stove."

Lauren smiled. Michael was being naughty, and she loved it. Their lips met in a soft, wet kiss. Michael's hands explored her body, stopping to take a firm hold on the cheeks of her behind.

Lauren let out a soft moan. "Let's not start something you can't finish."

"Keep it warm for me," he said in a voice so low it sounded as if Barry White had just entered the room. "I'll be back soon."

Michael gave her another gentle kiss and started out the door. "Oh, and forget about dinner," he said. "I'm taking you out tonight."

Michael walked out the door, and Lauren closed it softly behind him. She closed her eyes and allowed her head to fall against the hard maple door. *God, I love this man,* she thought. She just hoped that everything would work out, that they could somehow erase the past and start life anew. She closed her eyes tighter and started to pray, *Dear God, please help me find a way...*

"He doesn't have a clue, does he?" The voice coming from behind her was harsh and cold. "Poor ignorant soul."

Lauren whipped around and came face to face with Chance. He tried to take her into his arms, but she pushed her way free.

"I told you he knows everything," she said in Michael's defense.

"But does he know about us now?"

"There is no us now!" She was trying to keep her voice low, but the scream was building somewhere deep inside. "And what the hell are you doing here?"

"I had to come back to get my things." Chance said as he crept closer, watching her back away until she was pinned against the wall. "All of my things." He had an insane look in his eyes as he stared at her. That insane look told Lauren that when he said "all of his things". he included her in that sum. "I know it is going to be difficult at first, but you'll see. Our lives are going to be perfect. We will be the perfect family," his voice had an eerie tone. "Just trust me Roberta, everything is going to be just perfect."

Lauren looked up at him in shock. Was he losing his mind? "I'm not Roberta," she said, her voice filled with as much shock as it did with pitiful sorrow.

"There are so many lies and deceits in this world." He continued talking as if he didn't even hear her speak. "I think at the very least, friends should be honest with one another, don't you agree?"

Lauren slid her back against the wall in an attempt to scoot away from him.

"I mean we all are still friends, aren't we? And if we are, isn't it time that Michael knew the truth?"

The threat hung in the air between them, stopping Lauren in her tracks. She and Michael had just talked about pulling their lives back together. They had cleaned the slate and were off to a fresh start, and now here was Chance threatening to destroy it all.

"I think it's time for you to leave," she said.

Chance reached up and began to caress her, allowing his long, slender fingers to trace over her face and down her neck. "He doesn't really know you as well as I do," Chance said. "He doesn't really know the true passion that lives deep inside his sweet and lovely wife."

Frozen in a web of confusion, Lauren felt her chest heave up and down in short, rapid bursts. Chance continued to touch her, moving his fingers inside of the folds of her soft chenille robe.

"He doesn't know how to touch you in the ways you truly desire," he continued, shoving his hand between her thighs. "And I'm sure he has no clue what a hot little bitch you really are."

Lauren shoved Chance away with all her might. The push sent him toppling backwards, slipping on the smooth tile floor and landing flat on his back. She took off running down the hall, her mind searching frantically for some sort of direction. Chance pulled himself up slowly as he tried to regain his composure. The two of them had played many games in the past. She had been the bitch, the whore, the submissive servant, the dominating queen and the frightened little girl. She had played hard-to-get just the other night and had wound up begging him to thrust deeper inside of her. It was impossible for her to change into this totally dedicated wife in just those few short hours. *Has she forgotten all that we mean to each other?* Chance wondered.

"Oh, so it's like that now, huh?" Chance said as he followed her toward the kitchen.

Lauren grabbed the phone that hung next to the refrigerator. Her hands trembled as she stared blankly at the pad of illuminated numbers. Her mind was racing a thousand miles a minute. Who could she call? What would she say? How could she explain her sudden fear of this man who had been a friend for so long? She heard Chance's footsteps slowly approach. Her hand shook uncontrollably as her finger reached out to depress the illuminated buttons. 9-1...

Chance casually walked into the kitchen. His eyes bore right through her as he strolled up to the fridge, pulled open the door and peered inside. Lauren was just about to press the last button when Chance glanced up at her.

"Who you calling?" he asked indifferently. "Michael?" His

hands searched through the refrigerator as the words fell haphazardly from his lips. "You might as well, because whoever you call, it's all going to get back to him anyway."

Lauren listened to the dead air on the other end of the receiver while she stared blankly at the numeric pad, watching her own finger slip away from the number 1. Her mind was lost somewhere in a smoke-filled room with no means of escape. Chance pulled a long-necked bottle out of the refrigerator and twisted off the cap. The tinny sound of the small metal cap hitting the floor snapped Lauren back to reality. Chance took a sip off the bottle as he took the phone out of Lauren's hand and replaced it on the wall. He offered her the bottle.

"Thirsty?" he asked with an impish grin. It was the kind of grin people get only when they know they have the upper hand.

"I want you to get your shit and get out," Lauren growled.

Chance loomed over her like a haunting shadow. He was so close that she could feel his breath upon her face. "You don't really want to push me aside, do you?" he asked. His voice had that threatening quality again. "You're just confused and a little unsure about what you should do. It's Michael's fault. He's just putting too much pressure on you."

"What the hell are you thinking?" Lauren catechized, still trying to push him away. "You and Michael are friends. Best friends. Is this how you treat your friend? You need to leave me alone and try to reconcile whatever friendship the two of you have left. Michael knows everything he needs to know about us. And you should know that you and I are finished. I want you to know that it's over."

"And do you know what I want?" he said softly. "All I want is a day without pain" The look in Chance's eyes suddenly turned cold. His face hardened. The lines of his jaw became rigid. He turned his lower lip into a thin line and started biting away at the skin. "And I want Roberta back," he said through clenched teeth. "I want her back happy and healthy and waiting for the birth of our child. I want her back to stop the pain, and I want her back *NOW!*"

Lauren shuddered away from him, cowering in fear and shielding herself from his booming voice. In Lauren's mind, Chance had just stepped over the line of sanity. He had reached that breaking point when people snap and loose it completely. That point were human beings become their most dangerous and loose their sense of control, allowing their animalistic rage to take over. Lauren braced herself for the tirade, but instead of seething madness, Chance suddenly turned to her with an eerie composure, his face soft and tranquil.

"But I guess we can't always have what we want, now, can we?" he said. There was a sad peacefulness about him. He began to stroke Lauren's hair, allowing his mind to run free. "My wife is dead. My child is dead. There's nothing else left for me." Chance placed a gentle finger underneath Lauren's chin, lifting her head and directing her eyes to his. "You were there, you saw it happen. He took everything away from me. He owes me."

A single tear crept out of Lauren's eye. The dichotomy of emotions ran rampant inside her. She could see the pain that surrounded Chance. She wanted desperately to tell him that everything would work itself out. She wanted to hold him and to kiss him goodbye. But she knew that she could not reach out to him. They had stepped way over the line, and if she was ever going to get her life back together, she would have to make a stand. She was caught somewhere between terror and serenity. Lost in a paradox of bliss and pain. She felt the weight of the world as it shifted in her direction and knew there was no one to save her from this moment but herself. Her sad eyes connected with his. There was so much pain inside those eyes. So much anguish. She could feel the words "I'm sorry" forming deep inside, but what actually came out of her mouth was completely different. "Get out," she said. Her voice was strong and firm. "I never want to see you again."

Twelve

The Ice Hot Club had been the talk of the town since its inception. It was where the upscale people went to let their hair down. The kind of place where red-coated valets parked fancy cars and opened limousine doors, allowing jewel-covered women and well-dressed men to leave their troubles behind and stroll snobbishly toward the entrance. A thick red velvet rope hung across the doorway, where an elegant gentleman wearing an Armani suit checked to see if your name was on the list. Smooth sounds of live jazz tickled your senses, luring you inside.

"Right this way, Mr. Hubbs," the doorman said, then lifted the bright gold hook on the end of the rope to allow Michael and Lauren to enter.

Michael had pulled a couple of strings with one of his clients to get star treatment at the club. He knew he would end up owing the guy big time, but for a night like this, it was well worth it. The maitre d' led them to a small table for two right at the front and center of the stage. Lauren's smile danced lightly inside of her while Michael removed the colorful silk wrap from her shoulders and then pulled out the chair for her to sit down. He was into his "Billy D" mode and had a suaveness about him that she hadn't seen in years.

Lauren was wearing her favorite black dress. The one that clung to every curve and stopped suddenly halfway down her thigh. It was the dress she had designed for herself as a reward for all the hard work at the gym. A one-of-a-kind, Lauren Hubbs original, and tonight she was wearing that dress. At home she had wondered if it was too much, too revealing and a bit too sexy for a night out with the man she was supposed to be rededicating herself to. She thought about wearing something a little more frumpy and "wife-like," but from the moment she tried it on and saw the look on Michael's face, she knew this would be the perfect dress for the evening.

The club's sumptuous décor was a feast for the eyes, and the sound coming from the bandstand was music for the soul. A jazz quartet of keys, drums, sax and bass came together in melodic euphony. The young man sitting at the keyboard looked like a giant, cuddly teddy bear and had a face that couldn't have been more than twenty years old. But the way this kid's fingers tickled the keys, you'd swear the spirits of Theolonius Monk and Bill Evans had jumped into this young man's body and were holding a jam session with his soul.

Lauren's senses tried to take in everything at once. The sights, the sounds, the ebullience. She wanted to reach out and grab the moment, to wrap it up and seal it away in a box for whenever she needed a reminder of bliss. She was happy now. Happier than she had been in a very long time. It had been almost three weeks since that afternoon with Chance, and since then, neither she nor Michael had mentioned his name. *It was strange how he disappeared like that,* she thought. Occasional images of him still popped into her mind. She couldn't completely wipe away that haunting look he'd had in his eyes when he pinned her against the wall. She couldn't shake the feeling that he was always somewhere around-watching her. She could no longer take a long, hot, relaxing shower while she closed her eyes and shut out the rest of the world. Her eyes were always open now, constantly peeking beyond the steamy glass door to make sure she was alone.

As the band played, Lauren again had that strange feeling that she was being watched. She could feel Chance's eyes burning into the back of her head with that menacing contemptuous glare. She tried to turn her head inconspicuously, her eyes checking the faces in the crowd. She searched for that intense and sullen glare coming at her from some dark corner of the crowded room. But he was nowhere to be seen.

"You okay?"

Michael's voice had that deep raspy tone. It was that voice he used when he called her "Baby" and wanted her to know that everything was cool. She turned to him. Her gaze lingered on his face. Michael looked extremely attractive this evening. He had brushed his hair to the front, which made it glisten in undulating waves. He was starting to grow back his mustach,. and it was trimmed perfectly above his upper lip. His face had even thinned a bit, making those big, brown, fawn-like eyes of his stand out even more. Lauren could have kicked herself for allowing the mere thought of Chance to enter her mind on such a glorious night.

Michael had been so attentive lately, so caring. She even noticed it when the shapely "ho" of a barmaid had made sure to shove her 38Ds in his direction while leaning over to deliver their drinks. Michael had never taken his eyes off Lauren. He made her feel like she was the only woman in the room.

Michael and Lauren both took a sip out of the crystal flutes filled with sparkling bubbly. Lauren shuddered as the bubbles tickled her nose. They shared a smile and then turned their attention back toward the band. Michael put his arm around her chair and twirled small circles on her bare shoulder with his index finger. She leaned in closer to him. Snuggled against his side, she could smell the fragrance of his musk-sweet cologne. The scent was soothingly familiar. It ran across her senses and danced inside her head. She couldn't remember Michael wearing this fragrance before, but for some reason she recognized it all too well. Then it hit her. A wave of chills ran over her skin as if she had just felt an icy cold arctic blast. Lauren pulled away suddenly, realizing that the familiar scent was the smell of Chance.

"What's up?" Michael asked.

Lauren snapped to. She realized that she must have looked like she'd seen a ghost.

"What is it?" Michael continued.

"That cologne you're wearing," she said, trying to make her voice sound as light and inconsequential as possible. "Where'd you get it?"

"Oh, I'm sorry-I guess the least I could have done was to say thank you."

She didn't have the slightest clue what he was talking about.

"Your package, I got it at the office today," Michel said. "And I loved the card," he added. "'To remember me'—that was sweet."

Lauren swallowed hard and a lump that felt like a boulder went down her throat. Immediately, her eyes darted around the room. She caught a glimpse of what she thought was a familiar pair of eyes at the crowded bar, but the figure disappeared quickly.

The smooth sounds of the jazz band continued to fill the room, but now the music sounded like the dull ringing inside Lauren's head.

After leaving the club, Chance had walked around the city for hours before returning to his studio. He was still dazed with anger and confusion. He had come to some sort of understanding with Michael's behavior, come to grips with the fact that their friendship had run its course. It was obvious that whenever the two of them looked at each other they would think about what happened. They would both think about the catastrophic events and the image of Roberta lying on the steel platform in the growing pool of blood. It was apparent that Michael wanted to forget that image. To Chance, that realization became all too clear when Michael looked him in the eye with that holier-than-thou attitude and told him to get out. *How could he have forgotten?* Chance thought. *How could he forget the debt that he now owes?* He and Michael had come up through the ranks of life together as best friends. And, as with any friendship, best friends had a responsibility to each other. You lose my ball—you buy me another. You break my toy—you get me a new one. You wreck my car—you pay for the damage. You destroy my life....

Chance walked in a slow deliberate stupor through the massive open room of his studio. He had placed candles in virtually every corner and began to light each one with a long, thin, white taper he held with both hands. The dark room gradually began to glow with a flickering yellow luminescence that cast strange and eerie shadows on the walls. He glanced over toward the wall of monitors that displayed the random images of Lauren.

"Get on with your life," he said in an empty tone. "Evolve." *How does one evolve? How does one turn away from all that they have known and have embraced as whole? How do you leave the serenity of this day and walk into the darkness of tomorrow? Far be it from me to understand how one can rip out a soul that has been joined by a power much greater than I. To comprehend the powers that be when they decide what we have come to know is known no more. How do I turn and walk away? How do I evolve?*

Chance walked over to a thin metal pedestal that resembled a music stand, surrounded by a group of candles. On it rested a photograph of Roberta. He stared at the photograph, lifting it gently and bringing it to his lips. "How do I let go of you and in turn ask you to let go of me?" He placed a gentle kiss upon the picture. "The darkness of tomorrow beckons me. Calls me into its cold abyss with a promise of light." He lowered the photo slowly, holding it dangerously close to the flames. The heat of the candles began to crinkle the glossy finish on Roberta's face. "The future says that it is time to say good-bye. Time to change. Time to evolve. The time has come for us to say farewell and put aside that which man *did* find a way to put asunder."

Roberta's photograph burst into flames as he held it in his hand. Chance watched the burning picture, staring at the flames racing toward his fingertips. Something very strange was happening to him. His words rattled uncomfortably inside his own ears as if spoken by a stranger. What was with this Shakespearean Macbeth-like soliloquy pouring out of his head? The flames devoured the photograph and started gnawing at Chance's fingertips. He dropped the burning memory and watched the ashes float weightlessly to the floor. He turned back to the monitor wall filled with pictures of Lauren. "'Tis a strange potion this emotion knownst as love. It hast makest me start tripping harder than a motherfucker," he burst out in hysterical laughter, falling back into his billowy-soft chair. The electronic images of Lauren stared at him from across the room. His eyes locked onto hers intensely.

"My God, I need you," he said in a hushed whisper.

An Old Milwaukee beer bottle sat on the floor next to the chair. He picked it up and took a long swig, draining the bitter froth inside. The icy glass cooled his throbbing fingertips. It wasn't until then that he realized how severely he had burned his hand. He rolled the bottle slowly between his fingers and then pressed the hard, cool surface against his throbbing temple. His heart pounded against his chest as ice-cold droplets fell from the bottle down the side of his face. He was still transfixed by the images on the screens. A plethora of delusions flashed before his eyes. His hand holding the bottle fell limp and swung down over the arm of the chair, allowing the glass to shatter on the hard floor. Glistening fragments of broken glass sprayed upon the floor near his feet. Chance bent down, never taking his eyes off the wall of monitors, and picked up a shard of the broken glass. The sharp tip sparkled with reflected light. He turned the razor sharp tip of the glass toward his chest. A small moan of painful pleasure escaped his tight lips as the sharp glass ripped through his flesh. A trail of blood ran free as a flowing river as he slowly carved the letter "L" over his heart.

"I need you."

Lauren hadn't been able to shake the haunting feeling that she was being followed. She found herself constantly checking her back, whipping around at the slightest sound and cringing whenever footsteps approached. She could feel him out there—somewhere—lurking in the shadows. She could feel his piercing eyes watching her every move. He watched her leave for work in the mornings. Watched her walk through the empty parking structure late at night. She could sense his presence while she walked down the aisle at the market, and she could swear that he had watched the last time she and Michael made love.

Michael had laid her down in front of the fireplace in the den. He had kissed every inch of her body from head to toe and then he was inside her. They hadn't made love this passionately—this lovingly in a long time. The warm glow of the fire illuminated the room, and the two of them could actually see each other. The sight of their own sweat-covered bodies was an aphrodisiac in itself.

Married couples who have been together for years rarely make love with the lights on and usually opt for the familiarity and comfort of the darkness. But this time they were looking at one another. Their eyes were locked together in a needy continuum. That's when she felt it. All of a sudden she knew they were being watched. Her eyes darted to each window in turn, strained to see beyond the beveled glass of the French doors. Michael continued his rhythmic movements, but now she was distracted. He spent himself inside of her just as the loud shrill sound of a car alarm pierced the silence of the night. The shrieking siren echoed inside of Lauren's head. "Michael," she said. "I think that's your car." They both jumped up and threw on the nearest clothing at hand. Standing outside the house in the horseshoe driveway, they didn't see a soul, nor any evidence that anyone had been around. But Lauren knew he was there, and the resounding wail of the alarm on Michael's Land Rover continued to slice through the night.

He was there then and he is here now, Lauren thought, while sitting at the small sidewalk table. She and her assistant, Vanessa, were having lunch at a quaint little sidewalk café on Mullen St. Wrought iron tables with glass tops arranged perfectly on a small outdoor patio. Colorful market umbrellas shielded guest from an afternoon sun. Lauren sat with Vanessa, all smiles and girl talk, when the click-pssst of a camera made Lauren shoot upright in her seat. The sudden movement caught Vanessa off guard and forced her to also jump in her seat.

"What's up, girl, what'd you see?" Vanessa asked, her eyes darting around as if on the lookout for a swarm of killer bees.

"Nothing, I'm sorry," Lauren replied, trying to keep her composure. "I'm just a little jumpy".

"You need to chill out, girlfriend," Vanessa insisted. "Why you been stress'n so hard lately?"

Lauren looked around and noticed a young couple sitting

nearby. The woman was holding a tiny infant in her arms and a man standing in front of them was snapping away with a 35mm camera pressed to his eye.

"Looks to me like you're about one latte away from a nervous breakdown," Vanessa added. "Maybe you should give the Starbucks a rest."

"No, I'm fine," Lauren insisted. "It's just that for a minute I felt like someone was staring at me."

"Well, I should hope so. Two beautiful women sitting alone at a table without a man. You damn straight, they better be staring at us."

She gave Lauren a smile through brightly polished red lips that glistened like porcelain. Vanessa was very attractive in an exotic way. She was fair-skinned, even by her Puerto Rican standards, and her long, shimmering hair was the darkest shade of black. She stood only about five foot four in her highest heels and had a body that could stop traffic on a high-speed interstate.

She had a good point, Lauren thought. Why shouldn't the two of them deserve a few glances in their direction? She felt instantly relieved. Vanessa had a way of doing that for her. No matter how stressful things got at work or how impossible the task, Vanessa always had something comical to say and dove in with that "Come on, girlfriend, we can do this" attitude. That was probably the reason Lauren had hired her on the spot the day she came in after graduating from fashion design school.

Vanessa had dreams of becoming a designer and jumped at the chance to work for Ms. Lauren Hubbs. She knew Lauren was a young up-and-comer in the industry, and she would find no better place to get her fashion feet wet. She and Lauren hit it off right from the start. Lauren admired her brash attitude and boundless energy. The girl had what many of the buyers called *chutzpa*, and Lauren knew it would take this young, gutsy girl a long way.

Vanessa became Lauren's personal assistant, but much more than that, she quickly became a close friend.

Lauren paid the lunch tab, and the two women headed back to work, but not before stopping to greet the young couple and admire their adorable little girl.

With his briefcase and a cardboard cylinder filled with blueprints and plans in hand, Michael strolled quickly across the upper level of the parking structure. All and all, it had been a very good meeting, and he was proud to be on board. The council had looked over his preliminary designs for the new building, and everyone had seemed excited. He was finally going to get a shot at designing something significant. It wasn't just another towering building to be filled with dark suits and legalese, and it wasn't another stately home for some narcissistic, overindulged corporate muckety-mucks. This was something bigger, something that was actually going to do someone some good. It was to be called the Angel's Flight Building, a publicly funded educational institution for underprivileged children. *The Angel's Flight*, he thought. The name had a pleasant sound to it.

He was so caught up in his own thoughts that he didn't notice the bright-red convertible speeding by. He did stop instantly though, when he heard the screeching brakes.

"Michael?"

He heard the woman's voice calling his name and turned back toward the car.

"Michael, is that you?"

The young woman reversed the car at what must have been twenty miles an hour and sped backwards to Michael. She hopped out of the car and swallowed him in a huge embrace.

"Hey, you. It's good to see that you're still alive."

Michael pried himself out of the embrace and staggered a few steps back to a comfortable distance.

"Monica," he said with a noticeable discomfort in his voice. "How are you?"

Monica Richards was incredible. A cover girl's face with a centerfold's body. On a scale of one to ten, the judges would come back owing her change. Michael gave her a slight smile to try to hide his sudden uneasiness.

"It's been awhile," she said, sensing something was up. "What happened to you?"

"Happened?" Michael had just broken his first rule of thumb. He knew it was a cardinal sin to repeat any part of a question that someone had just asked you. In most circles, the redundancy meant that you were either stalling or about to come up with an out-and-out lie. He honestly wanted to do neither.

"Actually, a lot has happened. And I guess I've been needing to talk to you."

"So let's talk."

"I guess I should have called you, but I just didn't know what to say. I didn't want you to think that I was...you know -"

"Using me?" she asked bluntly. "The thought never crossed my mind. Besides, it was a mutual pleasure. As a matter of fact, it's something I'd like to do again."

Michael felt an uncomfortable rush surging through his body. In the back of his mind, he wished she would just slap his face and storm off. That would make things so much easier. Here he was, standing in front of what must have been God's gift to man, and he was searching his mind to try and find a way to kick her to the curb without hurting her too badly.

"I know there's no easy way to say this, but the truth is..." *Why am I pausing?* He knew what the truth was. Why didn't he just come out and say it?

"The truth is," he repeated, "I've fallen back in love with my wife."

Immediately, Michael braced himself for the fury that hell hath no equal to, but to his surprise, a warm smile graced her face.

"Well, well. How about that?" she said in a distant voice. "I was always under the impression that affairs were supposed to break up marriages." Although she hid it well, her pain was all too obvious. She was not the kind of woman who was used to being tossed aside for anyone, and the fact that Michael had chosen his wife over her was not doing her delicate ego any good.

"I guess I really have to respect your decision. I knew what I was getting into when - well, you know what I mean."

"I'm sorry. I..."

She placed a gentle hand to his lips, and her soft fingertips brushed against him lightly.

"Don't be sorry. Never be sorry for doing the right thing."

She embraced him once more, looked into his eyes and gave him a soft kiss on the lips. Michael took her into his arms and held her close. He could hear the soft, short suspiration of her attempt to fight back tears. He held her tighter, wanting to erase her pain. He didn't want to hear her cry. He didn't want to hear her crystal heart breaking inside her delicate chest. He didn't want to hear anything. And, perhaps because of that, he didn't hear the quiet *click-psst, click-psst* of the camera perched high on a nearby balcony.

Chance slowly lowered the lens from his eye while a sinister smile came over his face. He could hear the light whirl of the camera's motor rewinding the film back into the canister. His pulse quickened with the thought of his conquest. *Lauren honey, do you know what your dear, sweet husband has been up to lately?* The wicked thought tickled his senses.

Thirteen

"That's not my problem, Al," Lauren said into the phone. "I don't have a problem with the fabric. The problem is the fusing. And guess what—your company did the fusing!"

It was business as usual. A parade of people ran up and down the hallway carrying bolts of lace and silk past her office door, all of them talking at once. It was always hectic here; there was always some deadline to fill a buyer's order, or a rush to complete a line for a new show. The pace was always fast and furious, and with it came a constant pressure to deliver. She hovered around her desk sketching out a design for a new line of dresses, looking at samples of new fabrics, checking the deadline schedule on the office wall, and arguing all the while with the vendor on the phone. She had a pen in one hand a pair of scissors in the other and was trying to close the door to her office with her right foot with the phone clenched tightly between her cheek and shoulder. It was just another day at the office.

The telephone cord was just a few inches too short to allow her to reach the office door. She teetered with one foot on the floor, swinging the other in an errant attempt to kick the door closed. She looked like an epileptic ballerina as she finally grazed the edge of the door with the tip of her shoe. The office door slammed shut with a sudden *WHAM* that plunged the room into silence.

"I already know that, Al, that's why I called." The conversation was easier now that she didn't have to compete with the noise in the hall. "I need an answer today."

Vanessa entered the room carrying a huge vase filled with roses. The office door swung wide open, allowing the flood of noise to fill the room once again.

"What was that, Al? I'm sorry, I couldn't hear you."

She shot an annoyed look at Vanessa, who quickly got the message and used her well-rounded behind to push the door closed.

"Today, Al. I need an answer today. Call me back."

She went back to her desk and let the phone fall onto the cradle. Then she sank back into her chair with a long sigh. Vanessa set the enormous floral arrangement directly in front of Lauren.

"Stop and smell the roses, girlfriend," Vanessa said.

Lauren couldn't see anything but flowers. She tried to move the vase aside, but there was no space, and her desk was overrun with the colorful festoon.

"What is this all about?"

"I'd say it's all 'bout you, girlfriend. Looks like somebody's got a little som'thin special going on on the side. No wonder you've been so jumpy lately."

" I have no idea what you're talking about."

"Way to go, girl. When in doubt, deny, deny, deny."

Vanessa gave her that "You go, girl" look and then started out of the office. She stopped short of the door, remembering the envelope she held under her arm.

"Oh, I almost forgot this." She tossed the large manila

envelope on Lauren's desk. "It came with the flowers."

Lauren eyed the envelope on the desk. For some reason, it made her feel uneasy. It could have been anything—a new sample from a vendor, fabric swatches, a hundred and one completely harmless items. Yet she was afraid. The loud clamoring from the hallway started to fill the room again. She glanced up to tell Vanessa to close the door on her way out, but Vanessa had already gone. She wondered how long she had been sitting there staring blankly at the envelope.

She closed the office door, sealing herself in silence, then went back to her desk and studied the envelope more closely. Her name had been printed across the front in bold, black letters. The writing didn't look at all familiar. She flipped over the envelope and undid the small metal clasp. Her fingers slipped underneath the flap and then slid inside. She felt the smooth finish of thick glossy papers inside. A faint smirk of relief came to her face. *Must be a brochure of some kind,* she thought. *One of those artsy photo displays touting some vendors new and improved wares.* She hoped it had something to do with fusing. Al had really screwed up the fusing on that last order. The thick sheets, about ten in all, fell out in a complete stack, all of them upside down. She quickly turned the stack over and saw photographs of Michael and a beautiful woman standing outside in some parking lot, locked in an embrace and sharing a kiss.

She looked at the photos one by one, each one showing a more detailed version of Michael's apparent infidelity. Her breathing turned into shallow wisps. Her mind started to race, filling her head with a thousand questions. *Who is this woman? Is it her? Is it Monica? Is Michael still seeing her?* Lauren suddenly wondered why, when he'd told her apparently everything about the affair, he had never once mentioned how beautiful this woman was. She wondered where the pictures had come from. Who on God's earth would send her these pictures? And why? She continued poring over the photographs until she reached the last one, which she had to pry away from the picture before it. Some sticky substance held the two pages together, and they made a tacky kind of smacking sound as she pulled them apart. Lauren's face scrunched in a mass of confusion as she looked at the last glossy image of Michael and Monica. Scribbled across the photograph in large looping letters was the word "UNWORTHY." It wasn't the word that made her feel so uncomfortable. It was the sticky, dark, blackish-red ink with which the word was written. To Lauren, that ink looked a lot like blood.

Lauren felt the room spinning. Her head was weightless and there was a sudden disgusting taste in her mouth. The inside of her stomach pouded in constant heaves that echoed against the back of her throat. Lauren pulled herself from the chair, got to her feet and staggered out of the office. She felt as if she was on one of those fun house rides where the floor constantly moved back and forth, up and down. The hallway outside her office seemed to go on forever. *Thank God it's empty. Everyone must have gone to lunch,* she thought, bumping along the wall and making her way to the ladies' room.

Another wave of nausea hit her just as she entered the restroom stall. Her hands slammed against the cold surface of the stall's wall in an effort to brace herself while the contents of her stomach erupted in painful convulsions.

"Aaahhggg," she groaned over and over again until nothing more came from her mouth except a long, thin, translucent line of spit. Her legs were so weak that they trembled uncontrollably. Her knees gave out completely, and all of a sudden she was kneeling on the floor in the tiny stall. Lauren let her head rest on her arm, clinging tightly to the porcelain bowl. She couldn't help thinking that this was the same public toilet she couldn't bring herself to sit on whenever she had to go pee. Even when she spread the little toilet paper triangle on the seat, she still felt better squatting over the bowl without allowing her skin to make actual contact. It was ironic how different things were now that she felt deathly ill and was leaning her face against that same white, cool, soothing surface.

Footsteps echoed off the floor and walls as someone entered the ladies' room. Not the light, dainty clicks of a woman's high heels one would expect to hear inside of this female sanctuary, but thick and heavy footsteps that beat against the tile floor with a booming resonance. Lauren watched from underneath the stall door as the footsteps crept nearer. Her heart stopped cold when she saw the massive feet in wing tipped shoes enter the stall next to hers. It was him! Lauren knew it instantly. Chance had finally stepped out of the shadows and was there to finish what they had started. She should have known that it wouldn't be over so easily. She should have realized that he would be coming back for her.

Lauren struggled to her feet. She closed her eyes and tried to find some inner strength. *It has to stop now,* she thought. *All the stalking, all the hiding, all the phone calls where there is no one on the other end. It all has to stop.* Lauren checked once more to see if Chance was still there. *Of course he is,* she thought. *He is always there.* She ran out of the stall and burst into the one next to hers.

"Stay the hell away from me, you son of a bitch!" she screamed at the top of her lungs.

Lauren's face crumbled in an avalanche of embarrassment. No stalker was lurking inside the stall, no intruding man, no Chance. She closed her eyes and turned away from the large, angry woman sitting on the commode. "Sorry, Mildred," Lauren muttered, and then quickly walked out.

Lauren tried to go back to work, but her raging thoughts were getting the best of her. She had dumped the flowers and the photographs into the trash bin and had sat at her desk staring out of the window for hours. Before today, she had tried to write off the strange feeling of being followed as paranoia. But now, with the delivery of the photographs, she was sure that Chance was not only following her, but following Michael as well. She wanted to call Michael then and there to question him about the pictures, but she knew the questions would lead to more questions about Chance, and she didn't want to open up that can of worms. The nausea returned with a vengeance and sent her doubling over in pain. *Perhaps a visit to Dr. Black's office is in order,* she thought. *Maybe he can give me something to calm my nerves.*

Dr. Black's office was filled to capacity. Every examination room held a half-dressed woman going through the discomforts of some sort of exam. Lauren felt lucky that the nurse practitioner was on call. She agreed to give her a quick-once over. She grimaced as the nurse inserted two long bony fingers inside her and began groping around. She thought about how gentle Dr. Black always was and wondered why exams done by female doctors always seemed to be a more painful experience.

"Well, that's it," the nurse said, peeling off the latex glove and tossing it into the trash. "Dhere's no need to worry dere child. You might be getting an abdominal cramp here and dere, but de queasy stomach and da wooziness are all very common during de first trimester."

Lauren tried to cue in on what the woman said. She had a thick Island accent, like she was from Jamaica or maybe from Honduras or somewhere, Lauren supposed. She couldn't understand the woman and her words weren't making any sense. "First trimester of?" Lauren asked.

"Pregnancy, of course. Six to eight weeks would be my guess, but dere's no doubt about it. You might as well start picking out names and saving for college tuition."

Lauren attempted to get her thoughts together and her legs out of the stirrups at the same time.

"I would like to set up an ultrasound, doe," the nurse continued. "Jeez to rule out de possibility of a toobule and to make sure de lil' tike is nestled in dere just right."

Toobule? Lauren thought. *What the hell is a toobule?* "Okay..." Lauren was still numb. "Sure."

"You just finish dressing and den come to my office. We'll get your pre-natals and set you up for anudder visit."

The nurse walked out of the room, closing the door with a soft click. Lauren sat up on the side of the examination table, her mouth open in astonishment. *Pregnant?* she thought. *How in the world did this happen?* A hideous thought entered her mind and sent a stabbing pain to the pit of her stomach. *When did that episode with Chance on the stairway take place? Oh God,* she thought, *don't let this happen again.* She traced the steps in her mind more thoroughly. It had been at least a month and a half, maybe two since she last saw Chance. Her mind flashed back on that night with Chance. Then the next day. She recalled the time with Michael a few days later when he wanted to make love and she couldn't because...

The pain in her stomach started to drift away. Her memory was coming back, and she was feeling much better now. She dressed quickly and went in to meet the doctor. With pre-natal prescription in hand, she left the office and walked toward the elevators. As she headed down the hall, she stopped at a payphone and tried to call Michael.

Neither Janice nor Michael answered the phone, which flipped over to voice mail after a half dozen or so unanswered rings.

"Hi, this is Michael Hubbs. Sorry I can't come to the phone right now, but leave a message, and I'll call you back as soon as I return." Michael's voice sounded strong and sexy. Lauren smiled as she waited for the beep.

"Hey sweetheart, I've got some interesting news for you." This wasn't the kind of news she wanted to leave on the service. "Meet me at home as soon as you can. We've got a lot to talk about." Lauren started to hang up the phone, but quickly snatched it back to her ear. "Oh, I almost forgot. I love you." She hung up. A warm tingle ran over her and made her shudder with delight.

Lauren gave the button a second and third push while she stood there anxiously awaiting the elevator. She tried to think of some special way to let Michael know about the exciting change that was about to take control of their lives. Maybe she should greet him at the door wearing an oversized maternity dress. Or perhaps an expensive bottle of wine and a big cigar would do the trick. Maybe she could stuff a couple of pillows under her blouse and let him figure it out. Whatever it was, it had to be special. The rush hit her again, all at once. She was going to have a baby, and this was probably the happiest day of her life.

The elevator doors slid open and Lauren stepped inside the empty car. She walked on clouds. Her mind drifted a thousand miles away. *What do I want,* she wondered, *a boy or a girl? What will I name him or her?* The doors started to close, narrowing her view of the hallway into a tiny sliver. Suddenly, a powerful hand shot between the closing doors, forcing them to reopen. A bolt of terror ripped through her body, welding every muscle into one ridged mass. A scream started deep inside of her and lost its way trying to get out. This time she knew for sure it was him.

Chance stepped into the elevator, staring at her with cold, piercing eyes. The thick metal doors closed behind him, sealing the car like a tomb. Lauren closed her eyes, praying that he would go away. He came closer and stroked the side of her face with the back of his hand. He smiled.

"We've got good news, huh?" His voice was soft and peaceful.

"Chance, please."

"Aren't you going to tell me? I want to hear you say it."

Lauren glanced up at the row of glowing numbers over the elevator doors. The illuminated numbers weren't changing fast enough. She wanted the doors to open. To give her some means of escape. She tried to reach out and call for the next approaching floor. Her trembling finger rose discreetly toward the pad of buttons. Chance grabbed her hand and forced it down to her side.

"Come on, tell me. This is one of life's most special moments. Let's not screw it up."

"Let go of me," she said, trying to sound as forceful as possible.

"Oh, now is that any way to talk to the father of your child?"

The elevator came to an abrupt stop on the lobby floor. The thick doors slid open and Lauren was relieved to see a crowd of people. Chance might be crazy but he wasn't stupid. She was sure he wouldn't want to cause a scene.

"Leave me alone and stay the hell away from me!" Lauren shouted, snatching her hand away. She dashed out of the elevator and walked across the lobby as fast as she could without breaking into a run.

Chance followed, but Lauren felt safe. People were looking at them, watching them curiously, wondering what was wrong with the young couple. Lauren headed straight for the front doors of the building that led out to the parking lot. Maybe she could start to run as soon as she got outside, or maybe there would be tons of people around and Chance would just go away. As she came closer to the glass doors, her fingers searched inside her purse to find her keys. If she had the keys in her hand, she could make a quick dash to the car and hit the button that would make the car's alarm chirp twice and automatically unlock the doors. If she had the keys in her hand, she could hop inside the car, lock the door and hit the panic button on the remote to make the car's alarm sound with its screaming siren. With that noise blaring, someone was sure to come to her rescue. If she had the keys in her hand, she could hold the sharp, jagged metal between the folds of her closed fist and use it to gouge out his eyes, like she had learned in that weekend lesson on women's self defense. If she just had the keys in her hand.

Goddammit!, she cursed herself. *Gotta stop putting so much crap in my purse.* Her desperately searching fingers came up empty amid the loose change, lipstick, wallet, pens, scraps of paper and ATM receipts. Everything but the things she needed most. *Where in the hell are those keys?* For a brief second, her most frightening thought came to mind. *What if I left the keys back in the doctor's office? What am I going to do then, run all the way home?* She sighed with relief when her hand brushed against her jacket pocket and felt the jingling weight inside. With fingers wrapped tightly around the jagged assortment of precious metal, she walked confidently out of the building.

The parking lot was as barren as the Mojave. There were rows of cars, but hardly a living soul walking in the area. Lauren's mind went blank. She couldn't remember where she'd parked the car. Chance was fast approaching, and here she was, standing like a statue planted outside the door, not knowing which way to go. An elderly couple pushed past her, making their way into the building. Lauren looked at the old man with the walking cane, who was hunched over as if on a constant search for spare change. She knew he would be of no help when Chance came bursting out of the door. The image of the car flashed in her mind. *It's just across the lot,* she remembered, *parked between the old beat-up Oldsmobile and the brand-new light gray GS 400.* She ran as fast as she could across the lot, but just then Chance leaped out of nowhere and grabbed a handful of her long, braided hair. Lauren's neck arched back, and her body went sailing backwards, slamming against the hard brick wall of the building.

"You should know better than to run from me. It makes me very angry when you run." His words bore the weight of a dark and painful past. He'd heard those words said to him for many years.

"Why are you doing this?" Lauren was almost in tears. "Why can't you just leave us alone?"

"And walk away from my child?"

"I am not carrying your child, believe me. This is Michael's baby." Lauren's voice was confident. She remembered emphatically how relieved she was the day her period started after that last time she had been with Chance.

"Are you sure? Are you really sure this time? We'd hate for you to be mistaken."

"I'm sure."

"You know, there are things more powerful in this life than we could ever imagine. Things that you or I may never understand. The divine order of things."

Chance had a serene look on his face that could have been either inner peace or utter insanity.

"God may have had his reasons for taking Roberta out of my life," he continued. "Perhaps she wasn't the right one to see things through. But my child...I believe our divine father may have found another vessel to deliver my child unto me."

Lauren searched Chance's eyes, looking for some hint of rationality.

"Get some help, Chance," she said as she started to walk away.

"It's time for us to make some decisions about our future, Lauren. Time for us to decide what we're going to do about Michael."

Lauren came to an immediate stop. "This is between you and me. Michael has nothing to do with this. You stay the hell away from Michael!"

"My best friend? You want me to stay the hell away from my best friend and not share the exciting news that his wife and I are much closer than he thought? That his sweet, lovely wife may be carrying my child?"

Lauren's eyes narrowed into angry slits. "Whatever I felt for you, you've already destroyed. And believe me—if there was any possibility that this could be your child, I'd go back in that doctor's office and get rid of it right now."

Chance's hand shot out in an unannounced flash, coiling viciously around Lauren's throat. She gasped for air as his long fingers quivered against her soft skin. She could feel the veins at her temples pounding frantically.

"That is my child you're carrying, and if you even think about..."

Lauren's eyes were starting to roll back in her head. The world spun in and out of focus.

"Well, I think that's enough said about that, don't you?" Chance released his grip and allowed the oxygen to rush back into Lauren's lungs. She took in the cool air in short gulps, then shoved past Chance and staggered across the open lot.

"I'm watching you, Lauren," he warned, stalking slowly behind her. "Wherever you go, I'll be there-watching you."

Lauren banged her knee on the old Oldsmobile next to her car. Twinges shot down the length of her leg.

"What are you going to do, Lauren? Don't make me make these decisions on my own."

Lauren hopped into her car and slammed the door shut. Her finger automatically hit the button locking the doors. Chance charged the car with such force that it rocked violently. He pounded angry fists against the windshield.

"We're not finished with this, Lauren," he screamed. "Lauren! Get out of the fucking car, Lauren!!"

Lauren's hands shook so uncontrollably she was barely able to insert the key into the small slot.

"Lauren!"

The engine started with a roar, and she slammed the gears into reverse. The smell of burning rubber filled the air as the car shot backwards, almost knocking Chance to the ground. A millisecond later she was swerving out of the parking lot at mach speed. She blasted out of the driveway and onto the main street so fast that two oncoming cars had to screech to a halt.

A quick glance in the rearview mirror let her know the other cars were all right, but that more importantly, she was putting distance between herself and Chance. She grabbed the cellular phone from her purse, flipped it open and started to dial.

"911 dispatch," the tinny voice came on the line.

"Yes, I need to report a stalker."

"Are you in any danger right now?" The voice rang with concerned calm.

"Right now, I don't think so. I think I got away from him."

"Is he following you?"

"No—no, I don't think so. Look, I just want to place a complaint and have somebody pick him up. You can put him in jail, can't you?"

"I take it you know this person?"

"Yes." Lauren didn't see what that had to do with anything.

"And how are you involved with this person?"

"Excuse me?" The voice on the other end was working Lauren's nerves.

"Is this person a friend, a spouse...an ex?"

"I just want him put in jail, okay?"

"Yes ma'am, I'm just trying to get some information that will allow me to put you in contact with the right people. Are you currently involved with this person?"

Lauren didn't know how to answer that. There were too many questions. Questions she didn't care to answer. And what if they did pick Chance up? What kind of questions would they ask him? Her own twisted web tightened around her. Tangling her up in the lies and deceits. This was not how she wanted Michael to find out. Not through a probing police investigation. As a matter of fact, now that she was pregnant with Michael's child, she didn't want him to find out at all.

"I'm sorry. Never mind the call. It's just a misunderstanding," Lauren said and promptly clicked off the phone.

She sat at the stoplight on the crowded street. Her eyes searched every corner of the intersection. She prayed something went wrong with the emergency system so the police had no way to trace that call. She hoped no Petersburg cruiser would be speeding to her rescue. She wished with all her heart that the world would stop for awhile and allow her to sit right there and figure out her life.

The light changed all too quickly, and Lauren was snapped back to reality by the sound of a blaring horn from the car behind her. She drove on and decided to head home. Michael would be getting her message soon, and she wanted to be there when he arrived. No matter what was going on in Chance's head, this was still a wonderful moment, and she was determined to share it with Michael. She passed a small gun and ammunition store on her way home. She had never noticed the huge sign or the picture of the glistening Colt 45 before, although, she had driven down this street many times. She considered stopping, just to see what it would take to buy a gun of her own. She wondered how Michael would feel about her owning one. She thought about what it would take for her to actually pull out a gun and whether or not she would really be able to pull the trigger. She continued pass the small store without stopping, but, in the back of her mind, knew she'd return.

Fourteen

Michael was so overjoyed with the news of Lauren's pregnancy that he swooped her up in his arms and spun her around in giddy circles. He showered her face with so many kisses that she thought she would suffocate. Then he led her to the den, sat her gingerly on the sofa and dashed off into the kitchen.

"Just sit right there, Mommy, I'll be right back," he'd said.

He returned seconds later carrying a bottle of chilled wine and two long stemmed crystal flutes-the ones they used for special occasions. Michael couldn't stop smiling, showing more teeth each time he glanced over to Lauren. He uncorked the bottle, filled the glasses and joined her on the sofa.

"I guess there'll be a lot less wine in my future," Lauren said looking at the sparkling glass.

Michael grinned even wider and held up his glass for a toast. "Here's to our new beginning. All three of us."

He started to touch the tip of his glass with hers but stopped just short.

"But before that, I have something I need to tell you." His face turned serious. "I saw Monica the other day."

Lauren's eyes squinted with a puzzled look.

"Monica, the woman I uh..." He was stalling. "The woman I had the affair with. I explained to her that what happened between us was a mistake and that it would never happen again. I told her that I was sorry. I told her how much I loved you. And I told her that you were the most important thing in my life."

Lauren was stunned. Michael had just put into words everything she needed to hear. He had explained away the woman in the photographs. He had shown his excitement and commitment to her and the baby. And he had just expressed his honest love and devotion to their marriage. Lauren threw her arms around him. She wanted to throw her cards on the table too. To spill from her guts the noxious secrets she held inside, making the two of them clean and whole. *The truth shall set you free!* The thought raced through her mind. But the truth had been buried by so many lies that she didn't know where to begin. Would it be necessary to tell the whole truth about how the affair began? Would Michael want to know all the sorted details? Would he ask what kind of lover Chance was and want to know the comparisons? And if he forgave her for the past, could he forgive her for that one final slip of infidelity? There were just too many questions and not enough answers. She justified to herself that this beast from the past was too much of a destructive demon to bring into this moment. One day she would find the courage. This was not that day. She just simply clung to Michael tightly, telling her heart that it was okay to stay silent, empowering her mind to turn away from the past and go forward without looking back.

Lauren and Michael lost themselves in the oblivion of a thousand kisses. They left the crystal flutes untouched and slipped onto the floor to make love in front of the blazing fire. The lovemaking was slow and sensual, filled with looks of devotion and endless kisses. They fell asleep wrapped in each other's arms, glowing from the warmth of their love and the heat of the fire.

Still, as Lauren slept, her mind did not rest...

Lauren tenderly stroked the side of Michael's face. She could feel the rough stubble breaking the surface of his otherwise satin smooth cheeks. Her hand continued upward toward his soft wavy hair and danced around every crevice of his ear. She moved on toward the crown of his head and was about to bring her hand back to his soft face when she stopped suddenly at the feel of cold, hard steel pressed firmly against his temple. She bolted upright and stared into the face of Chance, who had materialized at the side of the bed. Her mind quickly tried to recall them ever coming to bed. The last thing she could remember, she and Michael had   fallen asleep in front of the fireplace. *I must be dreaming,* she rationalized. But the moment felt all too real, and the gun all too deadly.

"Hey there, lady," Chance said calmly.

"Oh my God, please, Chance. No!" Lauren's voice came out in a desperate whisper.

"I'll stop if you stop."

"What are you talking about? Stop what?"

"Stop the lies, stop the deceit. Tell him the truth."

Chance engaged the handgun. The sliding barrel made a loud *click-click* that filled the room. Michael sprung up in the bed as if he had just been hit with an electrical prod.

"What the fuck is this?" Michael sounded a bit more annoyed than he should have for a man with a gun pressed against his head.

"Tell him, Lauren. Tell him all about us. And then tell him about our child."

"What the hell are you talking about?" Michael said, trying to move his head away from the gun.

"Tell him!" Chance shouted, his finger visibly straining on the trigger.

Lauren's gut churned with urgency. "Michael, Chance and I had an affair!"

Confusion, pain and torment hit Michael at once. His eyes blinked rapidly, trying to take in what Lauren said.

"And!" Chance barked.

"There is no and!" Lauren screamed back. "We had an affair and now it's over. And I am so sorry it ever happened!"

"The baby, Lauren. Tell him about the baby!"

"This is not your child, Chance!" Lauren's mind clung to that reality. "This is Michael's baby and there is nothing you can do to change that!"

A cold, dead silence sucked all life out of the room.

"You lying bitch!" Chance screamed, pulling the trigger.

Bang! The gunshot sounded like a small explosion. Lauren saw the flash of light burst from the gun's barrel and felt the warm splatter of Michael's blood splash across her face. The ringing aftermath of the gunshot grew louder inside her head.

"Noooo!" Lauren screamed at the top of her lungs as she sprung up from the floor in front of the fireplace. Orange-red embers glowed on the hearth. Michael sat up quickly beside her and took her into his arms.

"It's okay, sweetheart. I'm here. It's okay." Michael's voice was soothing.

"I'm sorry...I must have been dreaming."

Tis a thin line between dream and nightmare that makes us tarry lightly into this blissful thing called sleep, Lauren vaguely remembered reading the words somewhere. She trembled, still caught in the throes of the terrible dream. Her mind struggled with her heart once more, and this time there was no contest. The vow of silence was sealed in the growing pool of blood that she could still see vividly in her mind.

Winter came without much pomp or fanfare. No torrential rains or snowstorms were on the horizon. The temperature had hovered around the mid-seventies, and it looked like it would be a bright and sunny holiday, something people from this part of the world referred to as a Black Christmas.

After the traumatic nightmare a few months before, Lauren had awakened every morning, and gone to bed every night, taking a moment to close her eyes and say a silent prayer. She prayed for forgiveness. She prayed for absolution. She prayed for the health of her baby. But most of all, she prayed that she would never see him again.

In a way, during the months that followed, she felt relieved. She felt safe in the belief that God watched over her and would in no way allow her to be harmed. She became confident that the angels were on her side and had seen a way to steer Chance completely out of her life and let her and Michael continue with a peaceful and cleansed existence. She felt good that she and Michael had grown so close during these short months, and that they were both anxious and excited about the baby. She felt at ease. So at ease that this morning, she forgot to pray.

The Westbrook shopping mall was a hive of activity. Holiday shoppers jammed the walkways carrying bags and packages and Christmas cheer. A slow-moving line, more than a city block long, was filled with wide-eyed kids and stressed-out parents, all waiting impatiently to see the jolly old man in the red velour suit.

Michael stood at a rack of greeting cards inside the Unique Card and Gift Emporium. He laughed boisterously while looking at a card with a flashy, pimped-out, mack-daddy-looking Santa slapping hips in an exaggerated bump with a hip hugger-wearing chick in afro-puffs.

"Hey Lauren," he yelled across the store. "I found the perfect card for your brother and his wife."

Lauren replaced a vase she had been checking out and walked over to join Michael. She had a slight waddle in her walk, and the paunch of her pregnancy was really starting to show. Lauren looked at the card in Michael's hand and rolled her eyes in a wide arc towards him.

"Are you making fun of my family?"

"No, sweetheart, of course not," he answered innocently. "I'm just saying that if bell bottom, polyester, double-knit suits ever come back in style, your brother's definitely gonna have it going on."

"Okay—all right, get it out of your system now, because when Phil and Judy are here with us for the holidays, I don't want to hear one single snide remark."

"From me?" Michael said with the biggest eyes of innocence he could muster.

"You'd better not," Lauren warned.

Michael replaced the card and Lauren turned to go back to her shopping.

"Hey, Lauren," Michael called.

She turned back to him just in time to watch him strike a Travolta-style disco pose and go into some kind of seventies flash-back dance step.

"Ha, ha, ha, ha, stay'n alive. Stay'n alive! Ha, ha, ha, ha—"

Michael's off-key singing and the wild and off-beat dance made Lauren laugh so hard that tears came to her eyes. Her hand was going to the corner of her eye when she suddenly froze with a contorted look of terror.

Michael stopped dancing immediately. His eyes followed her gaze outside the open doors of the gift shop and saw Chance standing there, staring in the display window.

Michael and Lauren walked hesitantly out of the store and stood arm in arm in the crowded walkway in front of Chance. The three of them stared at one another without saying a word. It was a cold silence. A silence that stabbed straight to the bone and froze them solid like marble statues.

"Well, isn't this special?" Chance said with a dour smile. "And look at you." He smiled slightly, looking at Lauren.

Lauren could feel him staring at her abdomen. It was as if he stared right through her skin and looked at her unborn child.

"Naw, man, look at you," Michael interjected, trying to sound unaffected. "You look...different."

That was the understatement of the year. Chance had indeed gone through some radical change, and it wasn't a change for the better. He was harder-looking. More muscular, yes, but not the kind of tone you get from healthy workouts at the gym and well-balanced meals. This was the hard-core tone you would notice on a guy fresh out of prison. Dark rings circled deep-red slits beneath which lurked his cold and piercing eyes. His hair had grown considerably longer, and the artistic goatee he had always worn so proudly had become long and scraggly bordering on something that resembled a Fu-man-Chu. And that wasn't all. Chance had dyed his hair—all of it, including the hair on his face, a bright, hideous, grotesquely startling shade of peroxide blonde.

"It was time for a change," Chance said, his eyes lingering upon Lauren. "You know, to evolve."

Michael tried to push aside his discomfort. Regardless of how this strange man looked, it was still Chance. His best friend. His boy from way back when. Time had passed and the tumultuous waters had come and gone under the bridge. Somewhere deep down they were still friends. Someone just had to make the first move. Michael reached out and took Chance's hand in a brotherly shake.

"It's been too long, man." Michael said, taking Chance into an embrace.

They slowly parted. Chance looked a bit softer now. Some of the ice had melted in that exchange, and he and Michael shared a deep look.

"We should try and get together sometime. Hang out, or something." His voice sounded light but carried hints of darkness when he turned back to Lauren. "You know, like old times."

"Yeah, that'd be cool," Michael said. He knew it was never going to happen.

"Looks like we've got quite a few things to talk about."

Lauren hadn't said a word through the entire exchange. It was as though everything inside of her had shut down at once. Her body was still standing there, but her soul and spirit had abandoned ship and run far, far away. The thought went through hret mind—*Yes, ladies and gentlemen, pay no attention to the zombie woman, standing before you. Lauren Hubbs has left the building.*

Michael felt the discomfort oozing from Lauren and knew it was time to give Chance the brushoff. "Yeah, man, we have to do that. Just give us a call sometime and we'll hook up," he said in his best voice. "Maybe after the holidays, huh?"

"Why wait that long?" Chance interjected, hardly waiting for Michael to finish. "You guys are still having your annual Christmas party next week, aren't you?"

Michael and Lauren could have been knocked over with a feather. Their faces looked dumbfounded.

"Uh...yeah. As a matter of fact, we are." Michael knew there was no sense lying. They had been friends for too long. The Christmas party was something he and Lauren had done every year since they had moved into the big house. Besides, he and Chance knew too many of the same people. If he lied and said that they weren't having the party, Chance was sure to find out. "You coming?" He was hoping to hear a "No."

"I don't know—maybe." He smiled at them both. "We'll see."

"Great..." Michael tried to sound upbeat. "We'll hope to see you there."

There was a long silent pause. That uncomfortable moment when everyone has run out of something to say, but no one wants to seem rude and make it too obvious that they want to get the hell away.

"Hey, I've got to run. It was really good to see you two."

Michael and Lauren both released sighs of relief. Chance leaned in to give Lauren a hug.

"And I have to say that pregnancy agrees with you, Lauren. You look beautiful."

He moved in closer. So close that Lauren could feel his warm breath on the side of her face.

"And by the way," his lips touched her ear as he whispered softly. "How is our baby?"

Lauren tried not to pull back too suddenly. Her skin crawled, and she had an almost uncontrollable desire to spit in his face. But she restrained herself and pulled back slowly, planting a strained smile on her lips.

"Your house. Christmas party. Friday night," Chance announced, giving them both a pat on the shoulder then turning and walking away.

Lauren and Michael exchanged empty glances of dazed confusion. At least they could tell from looking at each other that it only *felt* as if their jaws had hit the floor in unison.

Fifteen

Τhe sounds of "Chestnuts Roasting on an Open Fire" and every other Christmas ditty could be heard far and wide from the party inside Michael and Lauren's home.

The house was filled with friends and holiday cheer. Colorful platters of festive foods adorned the dining room table: crackers and Brie, cheddars cased in deep-red wax, fruits and flowers on a gold-draped table. Guests in elegant attire gathered in every part of the house, huddling in groups and engrossed in lively conversations. Visitors everywhere picked up crystal glasses filled with sparkling wines. Smiles and laughter filled their home as Michael and Lauren shared good times with close friends.

"So what'da guys want?" a man in the group surrounding Michael and Lauren asked while placing his hand on her belly.

"A boy..."

"A girl..."

Michael and Lauren spoke simultaneously and then laughed.

"Whatever, we just want a healthy baby," Lauren said.

"Good answer," Michael chimed. "A healthy baby, as long as it grows up healthy and happy, plays little league baseball, Pop Warner football and helps me out in the garage on Saturday afternoons."

"What do you have to say about that?" another guest asked Lauren.

"Sounds like our daughter is going to be one well-rounded individual," she said with a huge grin.

In another room, party guests danced to the most soulful rendition of "Rudolph the Red-Nosed Reindeer" ever recorded, compliments of the mighty, mighty, tempting Temptations. The dance floor was packed, and although a few of the guests risked hurting themselves while whipping out some of their old "Soul Train" moves, for the most part, everyone was having a damn good time.

Vanessa watched the party activity while perched on the arm of the sofa. She talked nonstop with a girlfriend at her side, the two of them pointing and gossiping about every other woman in the room. Vanessa's date sat nearby and looked bored to death. It wasn't the party that was getting to him. It was all of Vanessa's yakking filled with "girl, no!" and "Look'at that ho!" and "You know he always was a dog!" that was pushing him over the edge. He felt like a trained monkey who was supposed to sit by the side of his master and try his best to behave. Vanessa took a breath in her conversation long enough to catch him eyeing another woman and popped him upside the head so hard that it got the attention of everyone in the party. The two of them argued for the next forty-five minutes.

A few of the other party guests separated themselves to join Michael and Lauren in decorating the Christmas tree. It was at least stood fifteen feet high and had a base wider than a Yugo. A few friends couldn't help commenting on how many gifts it was going to take to fill up the bottom of that tree.

"Santa must be putting in some serious overtime in this house," one of them commented, placing another glistening red bulb on the tree.

As they decorated, someone started singing "The Twelve Days of Christmas," but the singing came to a grinding halt when no one could remember anything past "five golden rings."

By a quarter past ten, the party was in full swing. It was obvious that at least a third of the guests would be breaking the stringent holiday drinking and driving laws by the end of the evening. Vanessa and her date were at it again, arguing in a hidden corner of the house. The end of the argument had her date storming off for a vindictive dance with the young lady he had found so attractive earlier in the evening. Vanessa attempted to play it off as if it didn't faze her, but inside she was fuming.

Uncle Bill, a huge wall of a man who was darker than night and wore a bright red Santa hat, climbed onto an antique chair in the living room. He looked like the quintessence of having "one too many" as he tried to call the room to order.

"Attention!" It was only one word, but his drunken lips slurred it so miserably that hardly anyone in the room understood. "Your attention please!"

He wobbled unsteadily on top of the chair, looking like one of those trained bears in the circus taught to stand on a large red-and-white-striped ball.

Lauren cringed with embarrassment as all the attention of the party focused on the man standing in the tiny chair. Michael rushed over, placing a firm hand on Uncle Bill's arm.

"Uncle Bill," he said firmly. "We talked about the furniture— remember?"

It was true. Every year, since Michael and Lauren had started throwing their annual Christmas party, Michael's uncle would suck down every glass of champagne he could find and then work his way to the brandy-filled eggnog. And every year, near the end of the evening, good ol' Uncle Bill would have slobbered on too many friends, pinched some young girl's behind and found some reason to climb on some piece of furniture to make some obscure announcement. This year was no different.

"Relax, Mikey, I'm doing this for you," Uncle Bill said, getting too close to Michael's face. The fumes from his breath could have knocked out a horse. "Your attention please!"

Everyone at the party started to gather around.

"Thank you," he continued. "Lauren, my love, grace us with your beautifulness over here, would you please?"

Lauren joined Michael at Uncle Bill's side. He swallowed them both in a bear hug and then looked affectionately into their eyes. Lauren turned her head slightly and pressed her hand to her nose, trying to filter out some of the inebriating fumes spilling from Uncle Bill's pores.

"Ya gotta love these two, doncha?"

The chimes of the doorbell rang in the background, but Michael and Lauren had their hands too full of Uncle Bill to pay much attention. Vanessa gave Lauren a nod from across the room and went off to answer the door.

"Something makes me think back to the time when the two of you got married," Uncle Bill said, gearing up for a long stroll down memory lane. He drained the last drop from his glass and then looked at it as if suddenly enlightened. "It's probably the champagne! There was a lot of champagne when you guys got married."

"Uncle Bill," Lauren tried.

"You two had nothing!" he cut her off, raising his finger in the air as if to make a strong point. His finger hung up there for more than fifteen unanswered seconds while an amnesiac stare blanked out his face.

"Well, thank you very much, Uncle Bill," Michael said, trying to fill the silence. "That was a wonderful speech."

Once again Michael attempted to pull Uncle Bill down from the chair.

"Nothing but the hopes and dreams and blind happiness of a young couple," he finished, as if he had never stopped. "I told you then to enjoy that happiness because the longer you're married, the less of it you're gonna see. But you two have proven me wrong."

Michael gave Lauren a helpless look. Uncle Bill was on a roll now, and there was nothing either one of them could do except hold on for the ride.

Vanessa glided across the foyer heading for the front door. She paused briefly in front of a mirror hanging near the door to check her reflection. She started to primp but everything was in its place. *Forget that fool girl,* she thought to herself. *He just don't know what he's loosing.*

The chimes of the doorbell rang once more to remind Vanessa of her original mission. She swung the door open, and a bright smile overtook her face. There was Chance standing on the front porch. He was dressed in black, shiny leather that clung tightly to his muscular body. The bright blonde hair on his head and face were in shocking contrast to his ebony skin. He looked wild and dangerous. Vanessa was intrigued. This might be just the guy who would stand out enough to prove a thing or two to her ignorant-ass date who obviously didn't appreciate what he had.

"Well, hello there, Mr. Johnny-come-lately. Come on in and join the party."

Without hesitation, Vanessa linked arms with Chance and led the way into the living room.

The gathering crowd still hung on Uncle Bill's every word. His head moved wildly from side to side as he spoke to Michael and Lauren, making them duck each time he turned his head and sent the little white fuzzy ball on the end of his hat flying.

"And now into this nest, this den, this home full of love—the two of you are going to bring a child! And for that you deserve congratulations." Uncle Bill looked down at his empty glass. "I would toast you if I had a drink."

No one got the hint, so he cleared his throat as hard as he could and then repeated.

"I said, I would toast you if I had a drink!"

One of the guests got the message and quickly handed Uncle Bill a glass filled with champagne. Uncle Bill smiled.

"Now, some of you might say that this is just a cheap and underhanded way of getting another drink, and I say to you—It worked didn't it!" He raised his glass jubilantly. "To Michael, and Lauren and their new baby!"

The guests joined in with "here, heres" and raised glasses. Uncle Bill stepped down from the chair and pushed Michael and Lauren together, forcing them into an embrace.

"Kiss her, you fool!" somebody shouted from the crowd.

Michael and Lauren shared a tender kiss to the clinking of glasses and light applause from the gathered crowd. Lauren felt a warm sensation glowing inside. This was a good moment. One that she would remember for a long time. She looked out over the sea of smiling faces, taking them all in, and then her heart stopped cold.

An icy flood of adrenaline ripped its way through her body, freezing her in terror. Her eyes locked with Chance's crazed and contemptuous stare.

Lauren's body went numb. The wineglass fell from her hand and shattered on the floor in a fusion of shimmering glass and sparkling cider. She felt all the eyes in the room turn toward her.

"Sorry," she said. "I guess pregnancy promotes klutziness. Excuse me while I get something to clean this up."

She made a quick exit to the kitchen. Michael attempted to settle everyone back into the party mood and then went off after her.

"Are you all right?" he asked.

Lauren was obviously trembling, holding a dishtowel in one hand and trying to hold on to the kitchen counter for support with the other.

"I think I'm just a little jumpy." She wanted to ask him if he, too, had seen Chance, seen the way he stared at her. Seen his cold, empty eyes. She wanted to ask him, but she didn't. "Maybe I'm just tired, it is getting late."

Michael took the dishtowel from her and gave her a light kiss. "I'll clean that up. And let me see what I can do about wrapping up this party a little early."

It took awhile for Lauren's body to stop trembling. After she calmed down, she peeked out to the party to see if there was any sign of Chance still lurking around. She shuddered at the thought of what rumors he could be spreading among the guests. She dreaded the idea that she would see him huddled in a corner somewhere with Michael, telling him all about the dark and sordid past. She closed her eyes tight, trying to regain the strength to go back in to join the party. She tried to forget about Chance's bone-chilling stare. She swallowed hard and breathed deep and then a man's heavy hand landed on her shoulder.

Lauren spun around—eyes wide and fists clenched, ready to lash out and fight her way free. But the heavy hand belonged to the caterer, who was standing behind her. The timid little man saw the rage in Lauren's eyes. He withdrew his hand quickly and cowered in fear.

"Sorry Mrs. Hubbs! I didn't mean to frighten you."

"Don't sneak up on a person like that! You scared me half to death." She couldn't really tell him how she felt. How she was so glad that it was him and not the insane ex-lover she was expecting.

"I just wanted to let you know that it's getting close to eleven o'clock. We'd be happy to stay longer if you'd like, but our contract was for eleven—even though with clean up and all, we still won't be out of here before midnight."

"That's fine," Lauren sighed. "Whatever time you need, just add it to the bill. We shouldn't be much longer." With that, Lauren gave him a thankful smile and then headed out of the kitchen.

The party continued on until well after one in the morning, with guests trickling out in small groups. Lauren continued acting the perfect hostess, smiling brightly as people came to her to say goodnight.

"You're not leaving already?" she said to a bright young couple as they headed toward the door.

"Yes, I hate to go, but it's getting late and we've got a little one at home," the woman whined.

"And a sitter making five dollars an hour," the man next to her added.

"Well, thanks for coming." Lauren slapped on her Ms. Congeniality smile and walked them to the front door. As she walked, she checked over the remaining guests. There were only a few die-hards left, but more important, there was still no sign of Chance. She wondered what had happened to him. Whether the horror she wore on her face when she saw him there drove him away. *He was so angry and demented looking,* she thought. *As if it really hurt him to see me and Michael so happy at last. Maybe it did hurt him. Maybe he did run away, screaming madly in the darkness, and will never be seen again.* Lauren hoped the latter was true.

Michael had rounded up the last of the guests. He felt like a sheep dog herding its flock. As soon as he retrieved one straggler, another ran off from the group. Uncle Bill was the worst of all, stopping off at every unattended glass and draining its contents. Or hugging someone for the umpteenth time and bidding a sloppy goodnight.

"Dis here is the most booutifullest home I ever been in. And you two is the most bootiful people I know. I ain't never going home."

"Oh yes you are, Uncle Bill. You're going straight home and straight to bed," Michael said emphatically. He was carrying an armful of coats in one hand and steering Uncle Bill back toward the flock with the other. "Friends, it has been a wonderful evening," he announced, doling out coats and jackets to the aimless flock heading toward the door.

"Is this a hint?" a short, red-haired gentleman asked, receiving his coat from Michael. The little man's intoxicated face was as beet red as his hair.

"What hint?" the man's china doll trophy wife said coldly. "The man is handing you your coat. That's just as good as telling you to get the hell out of his house." She sounded like an irate waitress at a Chinese restaurant. "There's no more food for you! Chop chop, you go home now! Okay?"

Michael flashed his special charming smile. "No, come on. You know that's not true," he said, still pushing them all toward the front door.

Uncle Bill broke off from the group to go after another half-filled glass. Lauren beat him to the table and snatched the glass out of reach.

"Uncle Bill, I think you've had enough," she said sternly. "And I really don't think you should be driving."

"You wanna know some'thm, little darling. I don't even think

I should be walking." And with that, Uncle Bill crumpled to the floor like a wilted flower on a hot sunny day.

They all looked down at him and would have thought him dead had it not been for the deep guttural snoring sound rumbling from the back of his throat.

"I'll take him home," the little drunken redhead man grumbled, still struggling to put on his coat.

They all turned to him with astonished looks on their faces.

"I'm not driving. She's driving!" he scoffed, pointing at his lovely and completely sober wife. "Do I look like an idiot?"

It took four men to squeeze Uncle Bill into the back seat of the sporty two-door import. The rear end of the car sank close to the ground with the extra weight of Uncle Bill and sparks showered off of the dragging muffler as the loaded car pulled out of the driveway into the street. Michael wrapped his arm around Lauren's shoulders and let out a deep sigh of relief. They both looked up at the perfect sphere of lunar light hanging in the sky. The night was so clear that they could see the contrasting shades on the moon's surface, making it look like an albino version of the Earth.

They walked languidly back into the house, locked the doors and started turning off lights one by one.

Sixteen

"Tired?" Michael asked, watching Lauren survey the aftermath of the party. The caterers had done a wonderful job of cleaning up the place, but there were still a few assorted glasses and plates from the late-night guests that needed to be put away. She closed her eyes and nodded in agreement to Michael's question, and then started picking up plates, napkins and glasses and stacking them in a neat pile. Michael stopped her, ran his fingers through her braided hair, stopping at the crown of her head and scratched lightly. She purred like a kitten as his fingers soothed her weary mind.

A loud crash of breaking glass from down the hall made them both snap to attention. They gave each other perplexed looks and then turned their curious eyes to the hallway. *That sounded like it came from the den,* Michael thought. *But there is no reason for anyone to be in there. The room has been closed and dark all night, with the exception of a few people who had entered it by mistake while searching for the bathroom.* Michael and Lauren looked at each other. Without a word, Michael started down the hallway.

Lauren followed close behind, peeking around him like a frightened child.

The room was silent now. Michael pushed open the door and cautiously entered the darkness. As his fingers searched the wall to find the switch, he caught a reflection of something in the glass panes of the French door. He squinted hard, trying to make out the shape on the sofa facing the glass with its back to him. He could see the outline of something or someone laying, or hiding, on the sofa. He couldn't tell who, but he was sure someone was there. He cautioned Lauren to stay back, keeping her at bay with his left arm, still searching for the switch with his right.

He flipped the switch, filling the room with harsh light. "Why?" a voice cried out. It was a short and raspy voice and Michael was too startled to recognize it. He grabbed a champagne bottle that sat on a table nearby. Liquid splashed and spilled from the bottle as Michael brought it up over his head in one swift motion as though he was raising an axe. The warm, bubbling alcohol ran down his arm and spilled on the floor.

"Why does this always happen to me?" came a woman's voice. Michael and Lauren hopped back at the same time as the dark-haired shape sprung from the leather couch and turned toward them.

"Vanessa?" Lauren's voice rode up about five octaves. "What are you doing in here?"

"I needed someplace quiet to do some thinking."

Michael lowered his leaking weapon to his side, blowing out a long breath filled with tension. He then noticed a few other empty bottles in the room. "Did you say thinking or drinking?"

"What'dya mean?" Vanessa said innocently. She tried to walk toward them, but her wobbly legs wouldn't cooperate, sending her crashing to the carpeted floor in a drunken heap. "Okay, maybe I did have a little, but that asshole pissed me off."

"Who, your date? I thought I saw you sneaking out with him a long time ago. I was wondering why you didn't say goodbye. I just figured that the two of you must have been in a big hurry to get somewhere."

"That wasn't me that dog was sneaking out with. It was some skank-ass hoochie that he met here at your party."

"Wait a minute, that was your date?" Michael asked.

"You saw him leave?"

"Yes, and that 'skank-ass hoochie,' as you call her, was my secretary, Janice."

"Your secretary? Tell me where she lives! I'm going over there!" Vanessa struggled to get to her feet and slurred so much that she frothed at the mouth. "No, better yet, do me a favor. When she comes to work Monday morning, fire that bitch!" She made a wild gesture with her arms to accent her point and went sailing backwards over the sofa.

Lauren looked up at Michael. She wanted to ask him to take Vanessa home. See to it that she got into her house safely. But when she looked into Michael's eyes and saw the fatigue and frustration on his face, she held back the words.

"Okay, I'll take her home," Michael said, reading Lauren's mind. He started to help Vanessa to her feet, gathering her things while he pulled her up. "I'll be right back," he told Lauren. "And I don't want you trying to clean anything while I'm gone. Just go to bed and relax. We'll get this stuff cleaned up in the morning."

Lauren gave Michael a loving glance as he walked toward the car with the staggering Vanessa on his arm. He deposited her in the passenger seat, buckled her into the safety belt and walked around the car.

"I'll be right back, okay?" he said, blowing Lauren a kiss. "Happy holidays, huh?" He climbed behind the wheel and started the engine.

Lauren stood out on the porch until she could no longer see the glowing taillights of Michael's car. As soon as it disappeared around the bend, she felt an uneasy stirring inside of her, a desperate urge to call him back and beg him to take her along for the ride. She fought the urge, knowing that Michael would think that she was just being silly, and went back into the house. When she closed the front door, she gave the deadbolt an extra twist for good measure. The entire house was silent. Not peacefully silent, but silent like a mausoleum sort of silence. Her footsteps echoed off the walls, and for the first time since they had moved into this massive home, Lauren felt small and alone.

I'll just pick up a few things, Lauren said to herself, clearing a few more scattered items on her way to the kitchen. By the time she made it to the kitchen counter, she had her arms full of plates, glasses, silverware, napkins and a freshly-opened bottle of wine. She had no intention of ignoring Michael's warning about cleaning up the mess; everything just sort of fell into her hands as she walked. She chuckled to herself and then dropped the load on the counter next to the sink.

"Leave it," she said out loud to herself. Michael had told her to go up to bed and rest, and that was just what she was going to do. If she could just relax. Just unwind. It would take Michael at least forty-five minutes to an hour to make the roundtrip from Vanessa's. Until then she was trapped inside this big, empty house all alone. It never used to bother her, with Michael's long nights at the office and week-long business trips. But tonight was different. Tonight she felt the loneliness.

Lauren found herself removing a wine goblet from the overhead cabinet, and without thinking, started to pour herself a glass of wine. As she brought the glass to her lips, she stopped suddenly. *What am I doing?* she thought. *I can't drink this.* "The doctor said an occasional glass wouldn't hurt," she said out loud, pacifying her subconscious.

The cool wine lingered in her mouth and sent warm blasts throughout her body as she swallowed. One sip was all she need-ed to allow herself to give in to the exhaustion of the evening and fall into the waiting arms of sheer fatigue. She was just about to take one more sip when she suddenly felt the vice-like grip around the back of the neck. She tried to turn, but the clutch was too tight. The powerful hand pushed her forward, slamming her face into the overhead cabinet. The impact of the hard mahogany sent the room spinning. Lauren felt the wine goblet fall from her hand and heard it crash onto the floor. She felt the spray of warm liquid splash around her ankles as the hand released its grasp from her neck and grabbed a handful of her braided hair. Her neck arched back all at once from the pain of her hair being ripped away from her scalp. Then she felt the wiry goatee brushing against her face as Chance spoke.

"Haven't you ever read the warning label printed on those bottles?" Chance's voice was as frightening as it was calm. "It clearly says that you could cause harm to the baby." He whipped her around, forcing her eyes to his. "And we wouldn't want anything to harm *our* baby now, would we?"

Lauren jerked away. A small trickle of blood ran down the side of her face. She measured the distance between herself and the phone. She'd never make it. "Chance," Lauren warned. "Michael will be back here any second. You'd better leave."

"Do I look like the kind of man who would leave his child?"

"Stop saying that!" Lauren demanded, cupping her hands over her ears. "This is not your child!"

Chance took hold of the thick black belt he wore around his waist. The hard leather made a snapping sound as it slid from the loops of his pants. "Stop lying!" He screamed, slapping the belt on the counter just inches away from Lauren. "Stop lying to

Michael. Stop lying to yourself and stop lying to me. Didn't I teach you better than that?"

He brought the belt down again, and this time the thick strap landed against Lauren's hip. *Whap! Whap! Whap!* He spanked her like a child. Stinging, burning sensations ran down her side. Her hands struggled to catch the belt, his arm, anything that would stop the beating.

"Chance, I'm telling you the truth!" she screamed. "This is Michael's child."

"Liar!" he screamed back three times as loud. "You are mine now. That child is mine!"

Lauren shuddered uncontrollably with fear. Chance reached out to stroke her face. His eyes tried to lock in on hers. He was suddenly calm. Serene.

"He owes me, Lauren," Chance said with a tranquil air. "And now I am here to collect."

Lauren could taste the blood flowing down her lips. She sucked hard, getting a mouthful of the warm fluid, and then spat in Chance's face. Chance nonchalantly wiped away the spittle covering his face like a blood-laced web. Lauren raced across the kitchen as fast as she could. She reached for one of the large black handles that protruded from a butcher block on the kitchen counter. Chance swung the belt in his hand like a whip. The hard leather came down on Lauren's hand with a punishing smack. Lauren's hand quickly recoiled, and she rubbed the stinging welt that was already starting to rise. Chance bolted across the room and wrapped the thick belt around Lauren's throat.

"Don't make me hurt you, Lauren. I love you, but if you make me, I will hurt you."

Most of the ride had taken place in complete silence, with Michael behind the wheel and Vanessa staring out of the passenger window. They made a few attempts at small talk, but it was much too late, and Vanessa was far too pissed to concentrate on idle chatter.

"What the hell happened to all the good men?" Vanessa shouted. The outburst came completely out of left field, making Michael bolt upright in his seat. He knew that it was a rhetorical question, but nonetheless, felt compelled to answer.

"There's still a few of them out there. You've just got to look in the right places."

"Well, if you find one, you tell him about me," Vanessa said, trying to exude a confident air. "Tell him about this good woman who's sick and tired of dealing with all the dogs out there. You find me one, Michael. Find me a good one."

Vanessa pouted so hard now she looked like a little girl who'd been sent to bed without supper. She blew out a steady stream of air from her lips that made her long, flowing hair hang weightlessly in front of her face. Michael glanced at his watch, wondering how long it would take to get Vanessa to her apartment and return home.

"What about your friend?" Vanessa asked. "The one at the party?"

"Which one?"

"You know. The black blonde guy."

"Who, Chance?" Michael sounded a bit apprehensive.

"Yeah, that's the guy. Now there's an interesting catch."

Michael pursed his lips and made a sound like air escaping from a tire.

"Chance, huh?" Vanessa inquired. "I remember hearing about him. A friend of yours right?"

"Yeah, I guess you could say that," Michael mumbled.

"He was staying with you and Lauren for a while, wasn't he?" Vanessa asked curiously. "He staying with you guys again."

"Oh, no. Hell, no." Michael caught himself, not wanting to sound too hostile towards his former friend. No need to bring up a lot of unwanted questions. "He just stopped by the party to say 'Hi.' As a matter of fact, he didn't even say goodbye when he left."

"That's because he didn't leave."

"What?"

"He didn't leave," Vanessa repeated. "I saw him creeping around upstairs just before we left."

Michael's tires made a screeching howl as he spun the steering wheel in a perfect U-turn and headed back toward the house.

Seventeen

C hance backed off immediately when he heard the front door swing open and Michael's booming voice fill the hallway. "Lauren..." Michael called out. "Lauren, are you all right?" Michael charged into the kitchen to find Chance standing across from Lauren, who was lying on the floor. He noticed the trickle of blood coming from the corner of her mouth and the slight bruise above her right eye. His eyes then shot a piercing glare in Chance's direction. "What the hell is going on here?" Michael demanded.

"She must have fallen," Chance offered with limited concern. "I was just trying to help her up."

"Yeah, right." Michael didn't try to hide his skepticism. Had his wife not been lying on the floor just a few feet away, there would have been no question about the asskicking he was going to deliver Chance at that very instant. Instead, he pushed by Chance and went to Lauren's side. "I thought you left," he said to Chance, bumping his shoulder as he passed.

"It's a good thing for me that he didn't," Lauren interjected. "If he hadn't been here, I don't know what would have happened." Lauren could tell by the look in Michael's eyes that he wasn't buying it. "I feel so stupid," she continued. "I had just come in here to get a little sip of wine. I slipped—I hit my head on the counter, and cut my face on the glass..."

It all sounded a bit contrived to Michael. What was she hiding, he wondered? And why was she trying to protect Chance. His eyes shifted between Lauren and Chance. His mind trying to put the real pieces of the story together. There was obviously more to be said. A lot more. Michael helped Lauren to her feet, all the while never taking his eyes off Chance. "You sure you're all right?" he asked Lauren. She nodded, not wanting to say anything else.

"Did you forget about me?" Vanessa asked, charging into the kitchen. She stopped suddenly on seeing the three of them standing there. Immediately, she noticed Lauren's face. "Daaammmn, girl! What happened to you?"

"I just had a little disagreement with the kitchen counter," Lauren said lightly, forcing an uneasy smile.

"No shit?" Vanessa asked looking at Lauren's bruises. "Well let me tell you something, girlfriend. Not only did the counter win, that counter kicked your ass, and, if I were you, I wouldn't fuck around with that 'counter' anymore."

The air in the room was thick with tension. Michael looked over at Chance, who was returning his unwavering glare. "I need you to do me one, and take Vanessa home," Michael said to Chance. It wasn't a request; it sounded more like a command.

"No can do, partner," Chance returned. "I took a cab."

In a flash, Michael reached into his pocket, removed a set of keys and tossed them in Chance's direction. The keys flew like a bullet and Chance caught them coolly with one hand.

"Take my car," Michael insisted. "I'll pick it up tomorrow."

There were a few moments of unanswered silence. The tension

in the room continued to build like a burning pressure cooker waiting to explode.

Chance looked like he was deep in thought, but suddenly the thought passed. "Sure, no problem," he said, twirling the keys on his index finger. "And when you come by tomorrow to pick up the car, maybe we'll have a chance to talk." Chance looked right through Michael, his eyes glaring at Lauren. She obviously got the message. He snapped his head to the side and turned to Vanessa, "You ready?"

Without waiting on an answer, Chance whipped around and headed out. Vanessa gave Michael and Lauren a big "cat-that-ate-the-canary" grin and added a thumbs-up for good measure. "I'll fill you in tomorrow, girlfriend," she said to Lauren as she grabbed another bottle of champagne and headed off after Chance.

Chance stared out into the darkness, driving on autopilot as his mind reeled. He couldn't believe that he'd allowed such a perfect opportunity to slip through his fingertips. There they were, all three of them together. It was the perfect time to let the truth be known. But he had just stood there saying nothing, going with the flow. There was a brief moment when he started to tell Michael everything, but then *she* came in. She had barged in with her incoherent conversation and her drunken slur and ruined everything. Now he was stuck with her, driving aimlessly in the darkness.

Vanessa sat comfortably in the passenger seat eyeing Chance out of the corner of her eye. She blew lightly over the top of the open champagne bottle, making a soft, low, whistling sound. "So here I am with Mr. Johnny-come-lately," she said with a sly smile.

"My name is Chance."

"I know," she said turning to him. "I've heard a lot about you. Lauren used to talk about you all the time. I think at one time she was even trying to set us up. Kind of a blind date sort of thing."

Chance was staring straight ahead, not really hearing anything that Vanessa was saying.

"Well, anyway," Vanessa continued. "Here we are. Better late than never. Right, Mr. Lately?"

"I wish you'd stop calling me that and just tell me where you live."

"Don't worry, baby. You just follow my directions, and I'll get you there with no problem."

Chance was in no mood to play this game. *Who in the hell does this woman think she is? Doesn't she know I have bigger fish to fry?* They drove a while longer in complete silence except for the low, annoying whistle coming from the bottle.

Vanessa cocked her knees up on the seat, turning her body completely towards Chance. "I'm the kind of girl who believes when all else fails, go for the direct approach-so let me ask you something, Mr. Johnny-come-Lately..." She slid her body a little closer to him. "Has Johnny cum lately?"

Her hand fell lightly onto Chance's lap. Her fingers started to stroke the inside of his thigh and worked their way to his crotch. She leaned into him, bringing her lips to his ear.

"Would Johnny like to cum now?" she whispered softly in a low, sensual voice.

Chance's hand shot out, shoving Vanessa back into her seat. His forearm pressed against her throat, forcing her head deep against the headrest as he slammed on the brakes. Her body lunged forward, slamming her neck against his arm and cutting off the flow of blood to her brain.

"I think you'd better tell me where the hell you live and then sit over there and shut the fuck up." Chance's eyes were wild and fanatical. "Do we understand each other?"

Slowly, he lowered his arm, allowing the warm rush of blood to fill Vanessa's head once more. Her empty eyes blinked open and shut a few times and then turned to him.

"I think this is going to get ugly," she said with a blank look on her face.

"It doesn't have to," Chance warned.

"Oh yes it does!" she said as she leaned over and allowed the contents of her stomach to erupt into Chance's lap. Her body jerked violently for awhile, and then, the jerking tapered off to a sudden stillness. Chance looked down in disgust. He lifted her head to see the placid, peaceful look of the woman who was now out cold.

"Shit!" Chance moaned, letting go of Vanessa's head and allowing her face to splash back down into the mess she had just made.

Vanessa's head throbbed with a pressure that threatened to explode at the base of her temples. The harsh sunlight coming through the uncovered windows made her turn away like a vampire in the dawn's early light. She had a bitter, sour taste in her mouth and was groggy beyond comparison. The events of the night before were blurred together in a murky cloud of confusion. She looked around the room to get her bearings, but the only thing she knew for sure was that she was not at home.

"Oh man, not again," she muttered to herself pulling the thick comforter off her body and climbing out of the huge four-poster bed. The cold floor felt good on her bare feet. She pulled up the collar of her dress, which had fallen aside exposing her milky-white shoulders. Instantly, she realized it wasn't her dress at all. She distinctly remembered wearing the hot red skin-tight Versace that fit her like a glove the night before. But now she was wearing a crisp white linen shirt with French cuffs that were hanging well below her hands.

Her eyes combed the walls which were laden with pictures, black-and-white stills mixed with splashes of color. Some of it was very creative, even brilliant. Some of it was just plain weird. She stared at one particular black-and-white photograph of a woman in an old bathtub, one of those tubs made of cast iron with the big brass feet that looked like lion's paws. The woman looked as if she had slit her wrists and was lying in a tub of her own blood. A ghostly image of herself stood next to the tub, weeping. *This is some pretty creepy shit,* Vanessa thought to herself. She continued walking through the room. A flash of bright light and the sound of a whirring motor coming from another corner of the room caught her attention. *Click-psst, click-psst.* The sound drifted through the room. "Oh yeah, now I remember," she said, creeping towards the sounds and flashes.

Chance stood next to a camera mounted on a tripod. The bright strobe light on top of the camera flashed while he clicked off frame after frame of film. He was engrossed, entranced with the mannequin he had placed in front of the camera, posed strangely. The female form stood with its arms outstretched, the middle of its body completely vacant. It looked as if someone had taken a hatchet and torn out her wooden soul. Chance's eyes squinted into small slits as he concentrated on the form.

"Well, hello there," Vanessa said in a sultry voice.

Chance turned around to look at her. His face was rock-hard and unengaging. Vanessa offered a smile, but he gave her nothing in return.

"I guess I kind of overdid it last night, huh?" She sounded slightly embarrassed.

Chance allowed the long black remote cable to fall from his hand and slowly walked across the room. He headed toward a makeshift kitchen area, pausing along the way to flip the switch on the stereo receiver. Instantly, loud music filled the room with a deafening rage. Screaming classical arias plighted with painful resonance that sounded as if Jimi Hendrix had been reincarnated as a fat lady wearing a toga and a horned Viking hat.

Chance took a seat at a small wooden table that resembled an oversized butcher block. Vanessa followed him, checking out his physique from behind. *He is quite a specimen. Trim and muscular,* she thought, *rippling in all the right places.* She noticed how well the flowing silk robe clung to his skin, adding a smooth texture to his ridged body.

"That was some night last night, wasn't it?" she shouted over the music, still trying to lure him into some semblance of conversation. She strolled around the kitchen, making sure the crisp white shirt covering her body allowed him an eyeful of her alabaster skin. She stopped at a bookcase and reached up as high as she could, causing the shirt to expose just a hint of her well-rounded derrière.

It wasn't working. Chance was staring right through her as if she wasn't even there. Vanessa had spent the better part of her life being admired by men, having them fawn over her while she used her perfectly shaped body as a skillful tool. Men had actually groveled at her feet. Begged her for just a moment of bliss. And now here she was with this strange, disconnected man who was not giving her the time of day. She decided to turn up the heat a few degrees.

"So, tell me," she said, turning to face him head on. "Did I change my own clothes last night, or did I have a little help?"

"You were out cold," Chance said, so low that she could barely hear him over the music.

"So, I take it, you took my clothes off?"

"I had to clean you up. I had no choice, but to take off your clothes."

Vanessa took a peek inside the oversized shirt. The soft, round globes of her perfect breasts peeked back at her. "Everything?" She asked peeling the shirt aside slightly and giving up a hint of skin.

Chance let out a long sigh and turned away.

"So," she had that sultry voice working again. "Did you like what you saw?"

"I wasn't looking."

"Oh, come on now, not even a little peek?" Vanessa refused to believe that this body she had spent so many hours working on in the gym was not worthy of a little attention.

"It was dark."

She started unbuttoning her blouse and moving in closer to him. Surely once he saw what he was turning down, he'd change his mind. "It's not dark anymore," she purred. "Care to see what you missed?" She started to move rhythmically to the strange music. Letting her long hair flow over her back and slowly lowering the shirt off her shoulders. "You know, there's nothing like a little morning exercise to get you going...or coming, depending on how you want to look at it."

Vanessa moved with all the erotic ease of a lap dancer, teasing Chance with her soft flesh. Her hands started to roam over her body, enticing him, beckoning him to play along. She undid the last button of her shirt, exposing full round mounds and flawless skin. She was beautiful beyond description.

"What'da you say, handsome? Care to try a little Latin in satin?" She straddled him, slipping his robe away from his shoulders and pressing her breast against his chest. "I know more about you than you think, Mr. Chance Williams." Her lips were brushing against the side of his face, teasing his ear while her fingernails raked lightly along his back. "I know you haven't been with anyone since your wife died. Such a dedicated man. But believe me, baby, there comes a time in life when you just gotta let go."

Chance tried to push her away, but she was coming on strong, fighting his hands and forcing him to touch her.

"Climb out from that coldness and enjoy some of what the hot-blooded living has to offer," she said, shoving his hand down the front of her body and guiding him into her moist red satin panties.

Chance snatched his hand away, turning from her and staring across the room. Vanessa tried to guide his eyes back to meet hers, to no avail. Frustrated, she slammed her balled fist into his chest.

"What's the matter with you?" she demanded. "You forgotten how to get it up? Or did you bury that along with your wife?"

Chance's eyes whipped back to her. Glaring eyes that captured her in a heated rage. He slammed his hands on her thighs, squeezing them until she cried out in a rapturous squeal. In one swift move, he lifted her, swung her around and threw her down on the butcher-block table. Her back hit the wood with a loud thud, making her eyes widen and stare back at Chance. His face was stern and hard and his eyes were looking right through her. His hand strained against the soft satin until it snapped, granting him access to ram himself inside of her.

"Oh yeah, baby!" Vanessa shrieked. "Give it to me!"

Powerful thrusts, each one harder than the last. He was punishing her, and she was loving every minute of it. She clung to him, clawing his back, straining her lips to meet his. She wanted unbridled passion. He wanted pain. His hips moved forcefully, in complete defiance of her rhythmic undulations. His vicious jabs forced the back of her head to pound against the table.

"You know how I like it, don't you, baby?" Vanessa screamed, wrapping herself around him.

Chance's thrust became harder and faster as Vanessa's head reeled back, and she moaned in ecstasy. She never felt his hand slip away.   She never noticed as he reached out, his fingers straining to pull open the small drawer on the side of the table. And she never saw the glistening blade of the huge butcher knife that glimmered in the morning light. She just continued to hold on tight, her breath shortening to quick pants.   Lust, ecstasy and passion all about to explode within her at once. She drove her hips down hard to meet his as she shuddered and screamed in ecstasy — then in *pain.*

Vanessa's face froze in a horrible gaze lost somewhere between rhapsody and torment. Chance slowly pulled the long blade from her abdomen. The wound made a slurping sound as the metal eased its way out. Vanessa's head fell limply to the side. Chance lifted her face to meet his and looked into her empty eyes. A trickle of blood spilled from the corner of her lips. He used the tip of his tongue to lick it away.

Eighteen

The salesgirl behind the counter of the Shaford Jewelry Store carefully wrapped the oblong box in bright silver paper and finished off the package with a tidy red ribbon. She placed the gift on the counter next to Michael and offered him a big grin. "Your wife is going to love it," she said, slipping the small, narrow box inside a white and gold bag.

"She'll kill me if she ever finds out what I paid for it," Michael smiled back. He completed his signature on the sales receipt and handed the young girl both copies. *Good things come in small packages,* he thought looking at the long thin box that containing the sparkling four-carrat diamond tennis bracelet. He had just "Expressed himself" to the tune of thirty-five hundred dollars, but the look on Lauren's face when she opened the gift was going to be priceless. "But I think you're right. She is going to love it."

"Merry Christmas," the girl said in a singsong voice.

"Thanks," Michael replied. "And a Merry Christmas to you, too." Michael took the present and slipped it into the inside pocket of his long Bradbury coat. A satisfied look washed over his face with the knowledge that his Christmas shopping was done.

He walked out of the store into the heavy traffic of the mall's last-minute shoppers, a sea of people wearing holiday cheer as they pushed their credit lines to the max for those few moments of happiness. Michael thought about how special this Christmas was going to be for him and Lauren. It was their last Christmas of designer trees and expensive gifts just for each other. Starting next year, their tree would be laden with unbreakable child-safe bulbs; they would spend endless days in search of that perfect toy, and late nights trying to help Santa decipher the instructions for assembling the bright red wagon. A faded memory flashed in his mind of his father sitting on the living room floor, in front of the shiny silver aluminum tree, cursing to himself as he tried to put the scattered pieces of a tricycle together with a butter knife.

Michael smiled at the warm, rare memory of his father and then sat back as the cab continued to weave its way through the traffic. He was sure Lauren's brother and his wife had arrived at the house by now, and they would all be waiting for his return. He was also sure that Phil would no doubt be on his third drink at this late afternoon hour and already starting to badmouth him for not being at home to help his pregnant wife with last-minute preparations. He thought about calling to make sure Lauren was okay, but the tiny Motorola flip phone was still in the center glove box of his car. He only had one more stop to make before heading home and he was sure the stop would be brief. *After all, Chance and I don't have much to talk about these days. All am I going to do is to pop in, put an end to our friendship, pick up my car keys and go.* A new look quickly took over his face. A harsh and callous look.

Chance stood alone inside his dark room, transfixed in a world of insanity. The single red bulb jutting out from the wall cast strange, wicked shadows on his face. His bloodshot eyes looked dark and sunken as he stared down into the developing tray, watching the minute particles of metallic silver form on the papers lying in the chemical bath. Ghostly images were already starting to appear. Long dark hair. A pale and horrid face.

A loud buzzer rang out, cutting through the silence and jarring him out of his trance. His chest heaved as if he had been holding his breath for ages, and then he turned to the side. "I'll be right back, sweetheart," he said to no one in particular, and then, walked out of the room.

"It's open!" Chance yelled down the stairwell, walking toward the top of the stairs and drying his hands with a bloody rag. He tossed the rag aside, keeping his eyes glued on Michael climbing the stairs. "I guess you're here to get your car," Chance said with an expressionless face.

"Yeah, that and to get a couple of things straight," Michael said, arriving at the top of the stairs. The two men stood inches apart from one another. Each staring the other down in silent confrontation.

"What's on your mind?" Chance asked. The tone in his voice said he really didn't care.

"What do you think I am, blind or stupid?"

Their eyes locked for awhile longer, and then Chance turned and walked deeper into the room. "Well, you're definitely not blind," he announced, with a bitter sarcasm.

Michael tossed his coat onto a nearby chair and crossed behind Chance. "Look, man, I don't know what happened last night, and I'm not even sure I want to know. As a matter of fact, I *don't* want to know. But I do know that we've got some things to get straight."

"Maybe you should be talking to Lauren about this."

"I'm talking to you." Michael's tone was resolute.

"Okay." Chance shrugged. "Then talk."

Michael thought long and hard, choosing his words carefully. "You know, man, Roberta's death messed us all up pretty bad. It made some things difficult—like all of a sudden we didn't know each other anymore. Before that, you and me had always been tight. You were like family to me. You were my best friend."

"Interesting choice of words, my brother, *'were best friends,'*" Chance said scornfully. "Get to the point, Michael."

"Okay, here's the point. You and I ain't best friends anymore. We're not close, we're not family, we're not even acquaintances. We are nothing. I don't know what happened to you, I don't know what's going on between you and my wife, but I know I can't deal with it, whatever it is. I know you're trying to play me for some kind of fool, and I ain't going for it. The game is over. I can't play this shit anymore."

Chance's face went unmoved. "On a stack?"

The question had never sounded so final or cutting in all the years they had asked it of one another. *Would you swear on a stack of bibles?* He remembered asking Chance that day in the playground when they were both very young. *No doubt,* Chance had answered. *On a Stack.* It was the day that phrase became their call to honor.

"Yeah," Michael stabbed back. "On a stack." Both of them saw the sudden blinding flash of fifteen years of friendship wiped out in an instant. "I've got to start looking out for my family now. It's time to take care of my home. And you, my brother—you need to get some help."

"Is that it?... Cool, I'll get your keys now," Chance said, cutting Michael off. They stared at each other for awhile longer, and then Chance turned and stormed away.

"I'm serious about you getting that help, man," Michael called after him. "I mean, look at you." Michael's eyes combed the walls, pausing on some of the stranger photographs. "And look at your work."

Chance could still hear Michael's voice droning on as he entered the kitchen area. He was fuming, totally pissed that Michael could have the nerve to push him aside. Michael had never made amends for what happened to Roberta. He had never sought atonement for his actions. He had never paid for his sins. And now here he was, ready to charge off into the sunset to join his lovely wife with child and propose to live happily ever after. Was he some kind of fool?

Chance's hands rummaged through the drawer of the butcher-block table. He moved aside a few tools, a can opener, forks and knives. His fingers searched and landed on a set of keys, and then, he froze, staring down at the large butcher knife lying beside them.

Michael was still rambling on when Chance returned. He didn't notice how Chance kept one arm hidden behind his back. He never really looked back at Chance, since his eyes were still taking in the demented work that hung on the walls. "I really hope that one day you can find yourself again. Try to pull yourself back together..."

"Don't worry about me," Chance said with a half smile. "You've got problems of your own."

In a flash Chance whipped his arm from behind his back and held in his clenched fist...

A set of keys.

"How are you going to drive two cars?" Chance asked with a satisfied look.

"I took a cab," Michael returned with the same attitude that Chance had given him the night before.

There was an uncomfortable silence for a moment. "I hate long goodbyes. You know the way out."

Michael shook his head as he turned and headed for the stairs.

"And tell Lauren to send me a picture of the baby," Chance

called out, watching Michael descend the stairwell.

"Why in the hell would I do that?"

"I just want to see who the baby looks like."

Michael continued walking, not paying much attention to Chance's final words. "I don't think that's gonna happen," he said and proceeded down the stairs.

Chance stood painfully still, even long after he heard the soft click of the door following Michael's exit. His fists slowly balled into hard spheres and a low scream of pain erupted from deep inside. He ran through the loft, overturning everything in his path. He shattered pictures that hung on the walls, flung his photographic equipment down, shattering it into piles of broken fragments. He pushed over the rack containing the stereo receiver and CDs, and then stood in front of the bank of monitors where images of Lauren had danced at his beck and call. The monitors crashed to the floor with an earth shaking thunder as Chance stormed across the loft and kicked open the door to the darkroom.

The red light poured over the black walls in a blood-like luminance. Chance entered the room and stood in front of a poster-size photograph of Lauren. "I let him live just for you, my love," he said to the picture. "I let him live because I want you to be there when I cut out his heart!" Chance pulled out the knife from the waistband of his pants and plunged it right between the eyes of Lauren's smiling face. A frightening calm washed over him. His fingers traced the lines of Lauren's cheeks and around her mouth. "It's time, my love," he said in a soft and eerie whisper. "It's time."

Nineteen

The putrid smell hit Michael as soon as he opened the car door. A strong combination of booze and vomit that had taken over the car's interior and made it smell like the stench of a seedy skid row alley. Michael rolled down all four windows and drove with his head practically hanging out of the window. He thought the cool breeze would air out the car in no time, but the wind only made matters worse. The air seemed to drift into the car, scoop up a cloud of rank fumes and shove them straight into his nostrils. At this rate it would be a very long ride home. He pulled onto I-95, hitting the accelerator and looking forward to the burst of fresh air. But his jaw nearly hit the floor when he saw the cars stacked up ahead of him. The freeway was a parking lot of holiday traffic. *Should'ataken the street,* he thought. *At this rate I'll be lucky to make it home by Christmas.* The thought drifted through his mind as he glanced over to take another look at Lauren's gift.

"Shit!" he shouted, slamming fist of frustration against the steering wheel. The recollection hit him all at once. The expensive gift that he had just purchased for his wife was tucked neatly inside his coat pocket. And of course, he had left his coat—gift and all—back in Chance's loft. He pounded his fist on the horn, sending a loud howl through the air. He knew the noise was not going to make the traffic move faster, but he had to do something to vent his anger. There was nothing he could do but sit and wait for the traffic to crawl to the next off-ramp so that he could swing back by Chance's place and pick up his coat. He clicked on the radio, and the sounds of Donny Hathaway singing "This Christmas" filled the air.

Lauren glanced out the kitchen window over the sink, looking out onto the driveway for the fifth time in an hour. Michael had said he only had a few errands to run, but knowing that a visit with Chance was among those errands made Lauren feel uncomfortable. Chance had stepped way over the line, and she wasn't sure what he would say when confronted by Michael. The thought was too immense to dwell on, but she couldn't stop the questions from popping into her mind.

At least Phil and Judy had arrived. Their company eased her fear to a certain extent, and, at the very least, she was sure their presence would keep things from becoming too tumultuous if Michael did find out anything during his visit. Lauren carried two glasses back to the kitchenette table and placed one in front of each of her guests.

"Here we go," Lauren announced pleasantly. "A glass of wine for you and a vodka, no ice, slightly discolored by cranberry juice, with a twist of lime for my dear, sweet brother."

Phil, who bore a striking resemblance to one of the Temptations—complete with the powder-blue, bell-bottom jumpsuit, picked up the tall glass and guzzled down the drink in one gulp.

"Aaahhh," he sighed, placing the empty glass back on the table.

"Sookie, sookie now." The wide grin on his face gave way to the sparkling gold tooth in the center of his mouth. "Now that's what I'm talking 'bout! That was real good."

"How would you know," his wife Judy snapped, flipping up one side of her "That Girl" hairstyle. "It barely had time to hit your tongue."

As if on cue, Lauren picked up the glass and headed back to the kitchen to prepare another.

"Ah, Sis, don't trouble yourself," Phil said.

"I just thought you'd want another," Lauren chimed, already knowing the answer.

"I do. I just want you to save yourself a little time and bring the bottle on over here. That way you don't have to keep walking back and forth."

Lauren laughed and shook her head. She glanced out of the kitchen window once more, but still saw no sign of Michael. "Michael should have been here by now."

"Well, you know how he is," Phil said in his protective big brother voice. "The man's probably sitting up in his big ol' office drawing another one of them million dollar houses. He'll waltz in here two days after Christmas talking 'bout he didn't have time to get you no gift."

"I'll have you know that Michael is a changed man," Lauren stated proudly. "As a matter of fact, he didn't even go to work today. He went out shopping." She gave Phil a little smirk. "For me!" she added giddily.

"Well, whatever, the man is still late."

"Oh, Phil, give the man a break," Judy interjected.

Phil shot a look at her that would have iced over a brush fire. "Now, why you gonna stick up for the same man that dogged me out when I was wearing my Jherri Curl last year."

"He wasn't dogging you, sweetie. He just wanted me to follow you around the house and cover all the furniture with plastic before you sat down."

"Well, whatever. Point is, the man is still late," Phil said and took the drink from Lauren, who had just returned with the glass and bottle in hand.

Michael crept slowly up the stairs in Chance's loft. He had knocked, pounded and even yelled for Chance at the front door, but there was no answer. When he pushed the lever on the lock, he was surprised to feel the front door glide open effortlessly. "Chance..." he called out warily. "Chance, I forgot my coat, man. I just came back to get it."

He arrived at the top of the stairs and stopped instantly. The room was in shambles. Furniture had been overturned. Pictures had been stripped off the walls. The entire place was a wasteland of rubble piled on the dingy wooden floor. *What the fuck happened here?* Michael thought, retrieving his coat from the chair where he'd left it. He quickly checked to make sure the gift was still in the pocket. It was. Then, he turned to make a hasty exit. Curiosity was burning a deep hole in the pit of his stomach, but he was careful not to let it get the best of him. That same curiosity had killed much stronger cats than him, and this was no time to test his courage.

A slight rustling of papers in an adjacent room caught his attention just as he was about to descend the staircase. "Chance?" he called out softly. "Is that you?" He waited a couple of seconds, but there was no answer. He traced the sound to Chance's darkroom, a place where he knew Chance could hole up for hours working on his latest masterpiece. But that still didn't answer the question of what had happened here in the loft. Michael's mind told him to run, to get out of that place as quickly as he could. He had said all that needed to be said to Chance in their earlier confrontation, and there was simply no reason to hang around. But he ignored the premonition and crept slowly toward the darkroom.

"Chance—you all right?" Michael called, entering the room. It was pitch black inside. Waves of heavy black plastic covered the walls, soaking up all sources of light. Michael's fingers groped in the darkness and pulled a chain hanging overhead. The light jutting from the wall clicked on, filling the room with an eerie red glow. Suddenly, he felt that he was not alone. Piercing eyes bore a hole in the back of his neck. He whipped around to see Lauren's eyes staring at him from a huge photograph hanging on the wall. A massive rip ran down the length of her face as if someone had taken a sharp knife and sliced her head in two. "Jesus H. Christ," Michael muttered, staring at the picture.

More sounds of rustling paper made him turn around quickly. His face froze in a horrible mask as his eyes landed on the row of photographs that Chance had left hanging to dry. Bizarre and disgusting photographs of a twisted, contorted, but obviously dead Vanessa. She had been stretched out in front of a canvas and photographed as more and more of her insides had been cut away. The final picture showed the remains of the beautiful, young woman propped up near the mannequin, both of them with arms outstretched and completely void any midsection whatsoever.

"Chance, you sick fuck," Michael said, slowly backing away from the perverse art. An errant step landed him on a slippery spot on the floor, making his legs fly out from under him and sending him crashing to the ground. *Wham!* He landed flat on his back, his arm fanning out to break his fall. A warm dampness covered his fingertips. A slimy, sticky substance was leaking from a corner of the room. Chemicals, no doubt, Michael thought, lifting his hand to survey the damage. But the horror that met his eyes was all too repulsive. Dripping down the side of his hand and down his arm was a trail of blood. His eyes shot down to the floor where the dark red pool was spreading. Skittishly, he tried to get to his feet. The soles of his shoes slid frantically out from under him as he moved. He reached up and grabbed hold of the dark plastic hanging from the wall in an effort to gain his footing. The plastic gave way and a large, heavy object fell on top of him with a thud. He reached down to push it away and suddenly realized that he was holding the hardening corpse of Vanessa. Michael snatched away his blood-covered hands. Vanessa's blood. Her bulging, lifeless eyes stared up at him. Michael's stomach leapt to the back of his throat as if it was trying to escape.

Michael scooted out of the darkroom, frantically crawling backwards. He didn't stop moving until he reached the center of the ransacked loft. Bright sunlight filled the room. Michael's eyes shot over every corner. His mind was quickly becoming a raving maze of confusion, and he felt his sanity becoming lost in the twisted labyrinth. He saw Vanessa's cold eyes staring at him. Accusing him. Asking him, "Why? Why did you send me here with him?" He felt guilty about not taking her home himself and seeing her safely to her door. But soon another thought prevailed in his mind. Where the hell was Chance now, and what was he going to do next?

Twenty

The heels of Lauren's shoes clicked lightly across the marble floor as she raced through the foyer to answer the incessant knocking at the front door. She was sure that it was another UPS delivery or Fed Ex package from out-of-town friends sending late gifts. She dreaded receiving the late arriving presents which she invariably opened on Christmas morning only to realize it was from someone she had completely forgotten to buy something for from her mental list of family and friends. She cracked the door slightly and peeked out, expecting to see the dark brown uniform of a delivery person or the smiling face of the mail carrier. A hand forcing itself inside the cracked opening caught her completely off guard.

She tried her best to scream, but all she could manage was a pained gasp. Chance's powerful grip wrapped around her throat threatened to snap her neck in two. He shoved his weight into the door, sending it flying open, all the while still gripping Lauren's throat. She tried again to scream. The air blasted out of her lungs and stopped short at her throat, releasing a low-pitched gargling sound. Chance clapped the palm of his free hand over her mouth.

"Quiet now, sweetness," he whispered in a low soothing voice. "We wouldn't want to disturb the neighbors."

Lauren felt the room start to spin, her desperate lungs straining in empty gasps. Her body jerked violently, and, with all her might, she kneed Chance in the groin. He staggered backwards, giving her enough headway to slam the door closed against him.

BAM-BAM-BAM! Chance's pounding sent maddening echoes throughout the room. Lauren cupped her hands over her ears trying to block out the sounds. Phil and Judy charged in, their eyes wide and mouths gaping.

"What the hell is going on out there?" Phil asked, shielding his wife behind his long, lanky body.

"Phillip," Lauren said shaking her head in dismay. "Please don't ask me any questions about this, but there's a guy outside who I really need you to get rid of." Lauren knew the statement alone was going to pique Phil's curiosity and a third degree was sure to follow.

But the non-stop pounding and the booming voice on the other side calling out his little sister's name was all that Phil needed to hear. "What's to ask, baby sister? You want the guy gone, the guy is history!" Phil went into a nearby closet, rummaged around for a few moments and emerged with a long-handled golf club in hand. "Sounds like a nine iron job to me," he announced, heading to the front door.

The pounding stopped suddenly as Phil reached for the knob. Lauren and Judy backed away slowly. "Be careful, sugar," Judy cautioned, watching Phil peek outside the door.

"Be careful of what?" Phil said sarcastically. "Ain't nobody out here. The fool probably got scared and ran away."

"Oh, he's out there. Believe me," Lauren said.

Phil swung the golf club over his shoulder and marched

outside. He closed the front door behind himself, just to make sure the women were safe, and started to walk along the side of the house. "Uh huh. Running scared now, ain't ya?" Phil called out to the empty yard. "I got a little something for your ass you wanna come mess around here some more."

Phil continued walking around the side of the house. In spite of the angry, confident sneer on his face, his heart was beating a mile a minute inside his chest. As he reached the back of the house, all he could see was the quiet peacefulness that surrounded him. The massive trees that had given up their leaves to the winter. The sounds of the rushing water pouring over the rocks in the nearby river. The beguiling call of a loon as it glided effortlessly across a powder-blue sky. *God, this place is beautiful in a serene countrified sort of way,* Phil thought to himself. A twig snapped behind him. Phil whipped around in the direction of the sound. It was the last sound he ever heard.

Back in the house, a frantic Lauren walked to the den at the back of the house. "Maybe we should call the police!" Lauren said, starting for the telephone.

"The police?" Judy asked, pulling Lauren away from the phone and steering her towards a large overstuffed chair. "Stop worrying. Phil's a big boy, he can handle this." Judy placed Lauren in the chair and gave her arm a comforting squeeze. "Relax. You know how your brother is. He'd be offended if you thought he couldn't handle this on his own."

"I guess you're right," Lauren admitted, glancing up and seeing Phil standing at the back door.

Judy's eyes followed Lauren gaze. "See there. I told you he'd be all right."

Judy raced across the room and swung the door open. "What happened? Did you see anything?" she asked.

Phil just stood there, silent and deadly still. His eyes were open but seemed glassed over as if they could see nothing at all.

"Phillip?" Judy prodded as she crooked her neck slightly, watching Phil stand in the open doorway. Phil's body teetered back and forth slowly, like he was drifting in the gentle breeze and then, Suddenly, he fell like a mighty oak tree, slamming down on the carpeted floor. Immediately, both Judy and Lauren saw the large handle of a butcher knife protruding from his back.

"Oh my God!" Judy screamed. She fell to her knees next to Phil's body. Her hands trembled as she touched his back. The back of his shirt was soaked in blood.

Suddenly, Chance appeared in the doorway. The nine-iron golf club Phil had carried outside was now in Chance's grip. "Fore!" he yelled as Judy glanced up to see her attacker plant the cold metal foot of the nine-iron into the side of her face. "Mind if I play through?" Chance said, throwing down what was left of the club and reaching for the knife. Chance turned his angry glare to Lauren, who had already started to run out of the room. He pulled at the handle jutting out of Phil's body. The blade of the knife made a grinding sound as it slid out against the splintery bones of his spine. Chance looked up in the direction that Lauren had run off. "Lauren, I'm home..." he said with a huge grin. "And ya got some splain'n ta do!"

Lauren careened off the walls, running aimlessly down the hallway. She found herself standing in the living room before she was able to fight her way through the terror and begin to put her thoughts together. *A weapon!* She had to find a weapon to defend herself. *Something-anything!* Her eyes landed on the fireplace and locked onto the bright brass accessory kit on the floor nearby. She ran over and retrieved a poker, the weight of the stick felt heavy in her hand. Slow, deliberate footsteps headed in her direction. She quickly ducked behind the doorway, pressing her back flat against the wall. She tried as hard as she could not to breathe. Not to make a single solitary sound.

Chance crept down the hallway, stopping in the foyer to peer out through the front curtains. All was quiet in front of the house. No sign of Michael and no crazed Lauren screaming like a banshee up the front lawn. "Lauren, sweetheart. We need to talk," he cooed, wiping the blade of the knife on the sheer curtains. *The world is such a dangerous place now,* he thought. *Wouldn't want to pass on any germs.* There was a mad gleam in his eye as he turned and headed toward the living room.

Lauren shivered with fear. Try as she might, she could not control the labored breathing that escaped her lips in loud and heavy puffs. Chance's footsteps grew closer, until she could feel his presence on the other side of the doorway.

As fast as she could, Lauren lifted the poker and swung it with all her might. The heavy metal bar landed with a meaningless thud squarely in the palm of Chance's hand, and he snatched it easily away from her. Lauren looked at him helplessly. "Please Chance, no," she begged. "Please don't do this. I'm sorry. I'm so sorry!"

Chance's eyes were empty. No dancing light there sparkled with affection. No warmth shone through the windows of his soul. His eyes were as black as the darkest night and now housed nothing but cold-blooded evil. Chance shoved the heavy bar against Lauren's neck, slamming her head back into the wall and creasing the skin around her throat.

"Do you realize how much I love you?" Chance asked. His sincerity was staggering. A lonely tear seemed to form in the corner of one eye. They stood there for what seemed like an eternity, staring at one another. All the secrets and passion they once shared flashing by in a rush disjointed images.

The pressure on the bar eased up a bit, allowing Lauren to slowly move away. She held her back against the wall as she slid further and further out of his reach. Her eyes darted to the staircase.

"You forgot to say you love me back, you heartless bitch!" Chance raged, swinging the poker wildly and landing it inches from Lauren's skull.

Lauren ran frantically through the room, dodging Chance's swipes with every step. He was screaming like a madman. The blur of metal made a whooshing sound as it sliced through the air. Lauren ran back to the fireplace with Chance hot on her trail. She reached again for the accessory set, but Chance was there to grab her, spinning her around and groping for her throat. She swiped at him with one hand, clawing and scratching. With the other hand, she searched desperately for something behind her. Her fingers touched a cold, smooth plastic and her mind recognized the tool immediately. "Instant Match," she recalled Michael saying when he came home with the new trigger-like ignition tool used to light the fireplace.

By the time she got the lighter in her firm grasp, she was gasping for air under the strangling pressure of Chance's hands. She brought the lighter up in a flash and pointed it straight at Chance's face. With one squeeze of her finger on the trigger, the lighter clicked and spat out a stream of fire, searing the side of his face. Chance screamed and backed away.

Lauren sprinted across the room. She ran through the foyer and straight for the stairs, taking them two at a time.

"Don't run!" he screamed. "It only makes things worse when you run! Don't run!!"

She hadn't made more than six steps before Chance reached through the railings and snatched her legs out from under her. Her face hit the stairs with a thud, and all the air in her body seemed to burst out of her at once. Chance charged up behind her as she kicked and clawed her way free. Her long fingernails ripped jagged gashes across his face, driving him back. She turned and clambered wildly up the stairs with Chance in furious pursuit.

Chance heard the doors to the master bedroom slam shut. He methodically climbed the stairs with a wrathful look on his face. At the top of the landing he glanced down at the small table laden with photographs that sat in the hallway. He picked up the framed photo of himself, Michael, Lauren and Roberta, holding the banner announcing themselves as "The Best of Friends." A brief smirk passed over his face as he tossed the picture over the banister, watching it fall helplessly through the air and crash to the floor below. The image of Roberta came to him once more as he watched the photograph land and shatter violently on the cold marble tile. *A million shattered fragments,* just like his life had become.

Lauren was ransacking the nightstand drawer that had fallen to the floor, scattering its contents when the bedroom doors exploded open under the weight of Chance's boot. Her eyes met his as she scurried to her feet. "It's over, Chance," she warned. "You'd better go." She raised the 9mm handgun and locked him in her sights.

"You'd shoot me?" Chance asked wearily. "I give you my heart and you step on it? You're selfish...selfish..." He slowly walked toward her. "Is this what happens when lies and deceit blow up in your face?" He was yelling at her now. "You want to protect your perfect little life and you would kill me to cover up your lies?"

"Stop right there, Chance," Lauren warned once again. "Stop or I swear to God..."

"God?" he asked curiously. "You are my God!" Chance screamed, charging at her and grabbing the barrel of the gun. He forced the gun directly between his eyes as he yelled. "The Lord giveth and the Lord taketh away." He was ranting now. "Do it! If you want to kill me, do it!"

"Don't make me do this, Chance," Lauren begged. "I don't want to do this, but I will if I have to."

"My, my," Chance said smugly. "We are kindred spirits after all." The corners of his mouth started to rise. "But you won't do it. You can't, there's no way" he said as he tipped the butt of the gun's handle back in Lauren's direction. "There's no clip," he finished as he showed her the gaping hole in the base of the weapon.

Lauren returned the gun's barrel toward Chance's head and strained her finger against the trigger. "I said go away."

"There's no clip, babe. Don't you know what that means, sweetheart?" Chance continued. "It ain't loaded."

Lauren's determined glare melted quickly, and her arms started to fall from the purposeless weight of the gun. Chance smiled and snatched the gun away from her. He pumped the action on the barrel to check the chamber. A single bullet sprung out of the barrel and fell uselessly to the floor. Both Chance and Lauren stared down at the bullet.

"Whoa," Chance sighed. "That could have been ugly."

For a brief second, Lauren scolded herself for not pulling the trigger when she had the opportunity. *Should have shot first and asked questions later* she thought as she shoved the stunned Chance aside and charged into the bathroom. She tried to slam and lock the door, but Chance's weight was already pushing the door back open. She tried as hard as she could to force the door closed but his strength was too much for her. The door flew open, sending Lauren backpedaling across the floor.

"You're starting to piss me off, Lauren," Chance cautioned. He snatched her up by a handful of her braided hair and forced her to face the mirror. There he stared at their reflection. He stroked her shivering, tearstained face and gently nestled his cheek next to hers.

Lauren closed her eyes and thought about Michael. She thought about their lives, and she thought about the baby. *Oh my*

God, she thought. *The baby.* "Please don't hurt me, Chance. Please," she pleaded. "If you kill me. You'll kill our baby," she cooed. "And you wouldn't want to harm our baby, would you?"

"Our baby?" Chance's eyes lit up with hope. "You're now saying it's our baby?"

"Yes. Yes, of course!" It hurt her deeply to utter the dishonest words, but she knew it was her only hope. "This is our baby!"

Chance stared at the reflection of the two of them. He thought briefly what a strange looking family portrait this would make. The two of them with blood-streaked faces and demented eyes. Their eyes. Her eyes. Suddenly, he looked into her eyes and knew instantly that she was lying to him. "Liar!" he screamed. With all of his might he slammed her face into the mirror.

The glass shattered and splintered out like a web. Small shards clung to the front of Lauren's head, and trails of blood ran down her face. Chance flung her limp body across the room. He stared down at her, pulling out the large knife he'd tucked neatly into his waistband. "No more lies, my love," he whispered, raising the knife high in the air and charging toward her.

Michael heard the disturbance coming from upstairs as soon as he entered the house. He ran up the staircase, taking two steps at a time, and bolted into the bedroom. Immediately, he saw Chance holding the knife and heading toward Lauren who was lying on the bathroom floor. Michael grabbed Chance's arm and hurled him against the wall. "I thought I told you to stay the hell away from my family, you sick, crazy son of a bitch!"

"Give it a rest, Mike," Chance demanded. "You killed my wife, now it's time to return the favor. It's the least I could do. An eye for an eye, huh, partner? Ain't friendship a bitch?"

Chance raised the knife once more and charged at Lauren. Michael flew across the room and hit Chance with a flying tackle. The two men hit the floor tangled in an unyielding battle—fist and flesh tousling upon the floor. Chance's knife ripped painful gashes in Michael's arms and body.

Lauren started to fight her way back through the cloudy haze of unconsciousness. Immediately, she saw the two men struggling on the floor. "Michael..." she called out weakly.

The distraction was just enough to give Michael the upper hand. He landed a crashing blow across Chance's face and sent him reeling. Michael dove for Chance, grabbing the handle of the knife. The two men locked eyes in a test of will and strength, each trying to pry the knife out of the other's grasp.

The struggle moved into the bedroom, where Michael was finally able to wrestle the blade away from Chance. "Give it up, man," he demanded. "It ain't goin' down like this." Chance stared blankly at Michael. The memories of everything they had shared flooded his mind. His eyes became suddenly dark and sad. His face cold and stoic.

"It's the only way it can go down, my brother," he said with a distant expression. "This is all the family I have." And then he charged like a raging bull straight for Michael.

Michael stood his ground, holding the knife out in front of him. The knife made a squishing sound as Chance impaled himself on the sharp blade, forcing Michael to plunge the knife deeply into his abdomen. Michael watched painfully as his friend grew still and slid to the floor.

"Michael," Lauren called out, kneeling in the bathroom doorway. "I'm so sorry Michael."

Michael raced over to her, fell to his knees and scooped her up in his arms. "It's okay now," he said softly. "It's all going to be okay." He wiped away the flood of tears streaming down her face. He gently touched the wound on her head, which was still bleeding profusely. He wiped away a droplet of blood that fell on his hand. Then, another drop landed on her head. Michael looked at her curiously. *Drip*—another drop of blood. *Where the hell is that coming from?* Michael wondered. Slowly he turned his eyes upwards to see Chance standing over them. Chance held the knife over his head, clenched within his bloody fists. Blood glided down the smooth surface of the blade and gathered on the tip like medicine in an eyedropper.

Splat—another drop of blood fell from the blade and landed on Michael's face. In a flash, the gleaming, bloody blade sliced through the air and came down into his shoulder. Michael cried out in agony as he grabbed Chance's arms and tried to fend off the further attack. But the pain was too intense, and Chance was too enraged. Lauren screamed and lunged to her feet, racing across the room. Chance pulled the knife out of Michael's mangled shoulder and turned slowly towards Lauren, who had run over to the bed.

"And now, my love," he announced. "We all die!"

Lauren stood at the edge of the bed staring back at him. Their eyes locked once more, each of them seeing a place neither of them had ever been before nor ever wanted to visit again. "I don't think so," she said solemnly. Lauren raised the gun with one hand and aimed it directly at Chance. With the other hand, she slipped the black metal casing into the butt of the handle. "I found the clip."

The casing locked into place with a loud click, and Lauren took sharp aim. Demented anger returned to Chance's face. He arched the knife high in the air and wielded it like a mighty sword.

"Remember what I told you a long time ago about getting off of the tracks?" Lauren asked.

Chance made no reply and clenched the knife tighter. Every muscle in his body prepared to pounce. His jawbone tightened into a hard ridge and his temples throbbed.

"I think I hear another train coming," Lauren said.

He moved. Gunshots rang out like detonations from a small cannon. Chance's body jerked uncontrollably with each hit sending him backpedaling out of the room. The small of his back landed against the hallway banister, propping him up and giving him one last look at her. Lauren let her arms fall limply at her sides. She was just about to relax her hand and let the weapon slide out when Chance's eyes suddenly opened wide and the knife sprung back in the air. Lauren whipped up the gun and started firing blindly. Chance's body crashed through the banister, sending wood fragments flying. Lauren continued to fire the gun until she could hear nothing but the sound of empty clicks coming from its barren chamber.

Chance's body fell heavily through the air and landed with a bone-shattering force on the cold marble floor. A stream of blood spread quickly across the grand foyer floor, coating the marble tile and pooling against the broken frame and shattered glass of the picture of Michael, Lauren, Roberta and Chance—*The Best of Friends.*

Michael struggled to his feet. He fought past the pain and raced over to Lauren's side. She let the gun slip out of her hands and land softly on the carpeted floor. The two of them stared at one another for a long while, and then, lost themselves in an endless embrace.

Epilogue

"Y ou'd better run faster, I'm coming to get you!" Lauren taunted, chasing the small boy across the lush green lawn. The adorable little boy had just turned two years old and was quickly adopting the newfound thrill of running freely through the park on his own. Up until now, Lauren and Michael had been quite the doting parents, overprotective of their son, forcing him to lead a somewhat sheltered life. But since they had moved out here to the small, rural, Northwestern town of Santa Maria, they had vowed to start life anew.

Running freely through the park and enjoying the fresh, clean air was the culmination of that vow. Two and a half years had passed since the "accident", as they hesitantly referred to it. Things had slowly pulled themselves back together. But Lauren still had a hard time putting herself at ease. Back home she had been haunted by the feeling of ghosts lurking in the shadows. She still had the constant sensation of being watched. She knew that even after Chance recovered and left the hospital, he would be carted off to an asylum for the criminally insane and stay there for a very long time. Sources close to Michael and Lauren estimated that stay to be about twenty-five to thirty years.

Lauren still felt uneasy. She could no longer stay in the big rustic house alone. She avoided elevators completely, and shortly after the baby was born, she was easily vexed and became slightly paranoid. When Michael transferred to a different company and bought a small farmhouse in the quaint little town, Lauren welcomed the change with open arms and began packing immediately. Neither of them could wait to enjoy family Sundays together in a peaceful place filled with bright sunshine and warm afternoon breezes off the Pacific.

Little Jonathan continued to scamper at full speed away from Lauren's playful arms. His joyous shrieks came out in a piercing shrill that made Michael cringe.

"Well, one thing is for sure," Michael called to Lauren as she chased their son across the park. "The boy is definitely a screamer. A trait he got no doubt from your side of the family."

"Well at least he got something from me!" Lauren replied, continuing to chase the handsome child who was the spitting image of Michael.

Michael quickly joined the pursuit. A happy young family enjoying a day in the park. None of them noticed the rustle in the nearby brush or the quiet *click-psst, click-psst* of the tiny motor on the 35mm camera pointed in their direction.